My ~~twisted~~ Life In Middle School
Best Friends & Bullies

by Gina M. Wileman

Illustrated by Bob Longmire

First Edition

Eureka! Tutoring
Valencia, California

Library of Congress Control Number: 2020909502
Printed in the United States of America
ISBN: 978-1-7350855-0-0
First Edition: May 2020

Dedication

This story is a conversation starter…
For anyone who has ever been bullied at school or home,
this book is for you. If you are too embarrassed or ashamed
to tell teachers, parents, or friends about being a victim of bullying,
you're not alone. Try talking to God. Whisper—He'll hear you.
Eventually you will know, trust, and rely on Him.

Contents

Louie

Prologue

My name is Louie Pickle, and I've never read a chapter book in my life. Well, that's not exactly true. I've never enjoyed reading chapter books because I have dyslexia and get easily distracted by words. Some other kids in seventh grade might struggle with math, reading, or writing, but I actually love all of those subjects—it just takes me a little bit longer to understand what I'm reading. It's not because I'm dumb; actually I'm pretty smart, which is why I'm writing this book. Ba-dum-bum.

My friend, Nutty, and I have been BFFs since birth—*literally*. I mean, we were born at the same hospital on the same day in February. Mom thinks the stars were perfectly aligned that day, because now our families are inseparable.

And then there's Kent, my older brother, who's been jealous of my relationship with Nutty since day one. It's not my fault that our moms did everything together when we were growing up. For as long as I can remember, Kent has bullied me at home, school, church—everywhere. He seriously needs an attitude adjustment, because I'd rather not live the rest of my life with an ogre for a brother.

To make matters worse, Nutty and I are constantly getting teased at school. He's deathly allergic to peanuts and I'm lactose intolerant, so kids are afraid to sit with us at lunchtime. Apparently they're afraid to "catch the allergy germ." That's why Nutty and I have an agreement: (1) support each other *no matter what*, and (2) certain foods are *off-limits*, like chocolate-covered peanuts and vanilla ice-cream bars.

When you're an outcast at school, you don't have many friends. That's why meeting new people is rare, unless a miracle happens. I've been hoping Nutty and I will meet new friends this year—fingers crossed.

Some days can be more stressful than others, which is why I write poems to reduce my anxiety. I've never told anybody about them—not even Nutty—because my private thoughts are, well, private. Plus, they don't always rhyme. And I wouldn't want to offend people with my dry humor, even though writing about embarrassing things *does* make poetry more interesting!

Yesterday Mom said, "Louie, you need to exercise your brain instead of spending every breathing moment watching TV or playing video games." So I took her advice and challenged myself to write this book. Will anybody read it? Who knows. But if someone does, I have an important message:

Stop bullying me just because I'm different!

Life's too short to hide in the shadows, and that's why I talk to God sometimes. He understands me—even my dorky prayers—and I'm grateful that we're in this together.

Miracles happen every day, so never stop believing.
God can change things very quickly in your life.
— Anonymous —

1
This Big Nose of Mine

I have a problem. Whenever I look into a mirror, the only reflection I see is boring me—nothing special. Though Mom tells me otherwise. I've always been self-conscious about what others think of me since the only feature that stands out is this big nose of mine. Since it has a bump, Kent tells everybody that I broke my "oversized schnoz"—not! If only I could flatten this bony protrusion then maybe my nose would look smaller.

Even worse, lately Dad's been saying that my nose whistles. Really? As if the broken nose jokes aren't enough? *So what* if I have a blockage in my sinuses—big deal.

The other night at the dinner table, annoying Kent decided to poke a razor-sharp pin into my fragile self-esteem.

"What's that whistling noise? Does anybody else hear a locomotive train?" He roared with laughter and high fived Dad, who winked at him while trying not to choke on his broccoli.

My eyes squinted into slits of rage as my brain got hotter—like a volcano about to erupt in the kitchen.

"Be quiet!" I yelled, looking directly at Kent. "You're so immature!"

Dad upset me too, but I didn't look at him. It was an unspoken rule: parents are never at fault.

"Chugga, chugga, choo-choo!" Kent laughed hysterically. Everybody was laughing—even Mom.

"Okay, that's it. I'm outta here." I pushed my chair out from the table and needed a quick exit before the dreaded *tears* arrived. Dad

1

always said crying was a sign of weakness—I just needed to put on a happy face and pretend that nothing was wrong. I already felt pretty low, but Kent's teasing added another branch to my growing tree of sadness.

Kent knew better. He knew the difference between fair play and unjust cruelty. He also knew the consequences—that siding with Dad meant getting the silent treatment from me for a day or two. But he didn't care.

"Louie, sit down." Mom's sympathetic yet commanding tone acted like a vise around my ankles. She stood up and walked toward me, gently placing her hands on my shoulders. "If anybody says another word about Louie's nose, that person will be washing dishes every night for a week."

Mom to the rescue. Her words were like a cool spray of water dousing the volcanic flames.

"Anyway," she continued, "Grandpa would have loved knowing that Louie inherited his nose."

"Yeah," said Kent, "but did Grandpa's nose whistle?" Everybody laughed—but me.

Mom grabbed a dish towel and threw it at Kent. "Catch!" Mr. Varsity-Baseball-Stud reached up, like he was catching a line drive, and grabbed it. "Guess who's earned dish duty for the next seven days?"

Kent's jaw dropped. I bet he was imagining his personal life fading away. He spun around in his chair to face me and yelled, "This is all your fault!" Then he jabbed his finger at my nose. "If that thing didn't *whistle* while you ate, then none of this would've happened!"

Dad said nothing, which annoyed me.

Mom crossed her arms and frowned at Kent. "You've just earned yourself another week of cleaning dishes. Shall we make it three weeks?"

Kent was *furious*. He ran upstairs to his room and slammed the door behind him. Nobody moved. Silence. Then Dad excused himself from the table and went upstairs. We could hear whispering voices—mostly Dad's. Two minutes later, Dad came back to the table.

Kent followed closely behind, his tail between his legs. "Sorry, Louie."

"It's okay," I said, biting my tongue. I was willing to accept Kent's apology, even though he probably didn't mean it.

Dad must've talked some sense into him or reduced the penalty to one week of dish duty—lucky! Well, it's my turn to make dinner tomorrow night, and I can't wait to stack up a huge pile of dirty pots and pans in the sink for our new "dishwasher."

Only people who are not happy with themselves
are mean to others. Remember that.
— Anonymous —

2
Thick Skin Like a Rhino

I'm tired of everybody siding with Kent. Dad says, "Louie, you're too sensitive. Why do you have such thin skin? If you wanna survive in this world, then you'll need to grow thicker skin." Really? Well, maybe I was just born into the wrong family.

Maybe—instead of a human—I should've been a *thick-skinned* black rhino, because those four-ton machines can handle any bullies that cross their paths. If I were a rhino, I'd stomp through the South African grasslands without looking over my shoulder; every creature around me would tremble with fear and run for the hills. Even jet-black panthers with golden eyes would be trampled beneath my powerful legs. I'd push those scrawny cats out of my way like annoying fleas on my *thick-skinned* ear. That would be the best life ever.

I didn't feel like riding my bike to school the next morning, so Mom drove me. I sat in the front seat, miserable.

"Are you okay?" Mom asked.

I whispered, "I'm sick and tired of fighting with that jerk."

Mom was silent—she knew who I was talking about. Then she looked at me with smiling eyes and asked if I would do something totally out of my comfort zone. "Have you ever considered asking Kent why he treats you that way? Maybe you two should talk about it sometime. It could only help."

"No." I shook my head and said, "I would never talk to him, because the only words that come out of his mouth are rude."

Mom slowed to a stop at an intersection then said, "Then pray for strength, Louie. God knows how you're feeling, even before you say a word."

I didn't want to listen to her. It had been a while since I'd prayed, and I wasn't exactly sure how to do it. Could a simple prayer even help? But the fighting rhino inside me was ready to tackle my beastly brother, and since nothing else was working, maybe I should give it a try.

I turned away and looked out the car window. Then I closed my eyes and started to pray—without Mom knowing.

> *Hey God,*
> *I haven't a clue*
> *how to pray to you.*
> *Will you tell me what to do?*
> *If Kent irritates me till the day I die,*
> *then please send a rhino*
> *to gouge out his eye.*
> *But if you give him a nudge,*
> *and he's willing to budge,*
> *if he changes his 'tude*
> *and has a better mood,*
> *then maybe we can*
> *hang like dudes,*
> *like other brothers do.*
> *Please give me a sign;*
> *show me if I'm doing fine,*
> *'cause I think I'm going out of my mind.*
> *I know that might be asking a lot,*
> *but what the heck, it's all I've got.*

So it wasn't the nicest prayer, but at least I tried. And I felt much better afterwards.

I've often thought about having surgery to remove this giant bump on my nose. But after I researched it online, I found out that clobbering your nose and reshaping it like a fistful of dough is called *rhino*plasty. After the surgery, the doctor jams three feet of cotton gauze into your sinuses to stop the bleeding, and then, a week later, he'll yank the gauze out of your head. No thanks! That sounds too painful for me, but I do know someone who had it done.

Fiona's parents are rich, and they paid $15,000 for her nose job last year. Her new-and-improved nose looked great for a few months, until someone accidentally dropped a five-pound book on her *face!* I heard she was squatting down to get something out of her lower locker when someone standing above her dropped a science book—*bam!* People said Fiona's nose swelled up like a red balloon and she screamed all the way to the nurse's office.

After hearing that story, I decided I'm perfectly fine with the bump on my nose—for now. But the next person who teases me about it will feel the weight of my history book in their gut. And I'm willing to clean dishes for a week, if it comes to that.

Developing a tough thick skin is a way that we can guard our hearts from the wounds that cause it to develop a hard crust. I read that having a thick skin is being able to withstand criticism.
— With Devotion. KCBob.com —

3

Drink the Brain Juice

Positive self-talk has never been my strength. That's why it's hard to pull myself out of a funk whenever Kent criticizes me. *"Louie, why are you such a loser? Louie, why is your nose so big? Louie, when will you learn how to read like a normal person?"*

During lunchtime at school, Nutty and I always sit at the same table in the cafeteria. We usually vent about our lives.

"Why didn't I get a normal brother?" I asked him.

"You need to ignore Bobblebutt," said Nutty, inspecting his sandwich. "Don't let him get on your nerves." He started calling Kent "Bobblebutt" after we saw a baseball player's bobblehead figure at a second hand store.

"Easier said than done," I said. "He hates me."

"Louie, you've just gotta change the way you think about him." Nutty tossed his sandwich into the trash can next to our table. "Drink the *braaaain* juice, dude." He dragged out the word *brain*, making his voice sound like a monster from a horror movie.

I paused, carrot stick halfway to my mouth. "Brain juice? What are you talking about?"

Nutty laughed. "Last night, my dad heard me say, 'I hate math!' So he told me to drink the *braaaain* juice."

"What does that mean?"

"He said if I keep telling myself that I hate math, then I'll always hate math—until I change my attitude. Then it might not be so bad."

"Well, duh. That's a no-*brainer!*" Both of us laughed.

"But, really, Louie. My dad said there's a part of your brain called the subconscious mind. It believes anything you tell it, even if it's not true."

"No way!"

"Yup. So in other words"—he pretended to drink from an invisible cup—"I need to chug down some positive thoughts about math. That's what my dad told me."

I still didn't get it. "What does that story have to do with me?"

"Everything."

I took a bite of my tuna sandwich. "Okay," I said impatiently between chews, "I'm listening."

"Here's an example. Let's say you love pepperoni pizza."

"You already know that I love pepperoni pizza, dude. As long as my mom takes off the cheese."

"Yeah!" He laughed. "But what if you start telling yourself that pepperoni pizza tastes like maggot-covered meat with moldy tomatoes?"

I stopped chewing. "Ewww!"

"Exactly! Just the thought of eating pepperoni pizza will make you gag, because your subconscious mind will believe it."

I still didn't buy it. "There's no way that would happen," I said. "Pepperoni pizza's my all-time fave."

"Just wait until you try it next time!" Nutty winked and high fived me across the table.

"I'm still not sure this subconscious mind thing is legit. And how's pizza related to Bobblebutt anyway?"

Nutty reached into his backpack, pulled out some grapes, and popped a few into his mouth. He chewed—deep in thought—and then said, "Have you ever considered that maybe—just maybe—part of Kent's brain doesn't think he's doing anything wrong?"

My face got hot. "Whose side are you on anyway?"

Nutty laughed and pulled back. "Dude, no offense. But if Kent's

been bullying you since birth, and nobody's been stopping him…
I mean, *have* your parents done anything to stop him?"

"Well, yeah, sometimes they ground him."

"But you said your parents laugh, whenever he makes fun of
you."

"Yeah."

"Sorry to say this, but it sounds like your dad and mom are
partly to blame." Nutty shoved the rest of his lunch into his
backpack and stood up.

Could there be truth to that? "You think so?"

"Yeah, I do. That's probably why Bobblebutt's still allowed to
push you around. Your parents aren't comfortable dealing with it."

For a moment, I was speechless. "Oh, my gosh, Nutty. You
might be right." It felt like the walls and ceiling were closing in
around me.

"In the meantime," Nutty continued, "just drink the *braaaain*
juice. Then maybe Bobblebutt's words won't bother you so much."
Nutty slung the backpack over his shoulder and left for class. "See
ya in class, man."

As I sat alone in the cafeteria, I thought about the hundreds—
no, *thousands*—of times that Kent had insulted me in front of my
parents. The more I thought about Dad and Mom letting him
push me around, the angrier I became. I was too upset to drink the
so-called *braaaain* juice.

There were so many ways Dad and Mom could have handled
things differently. Why hadn't they done anything to make him
stop treating me that way? It was starting to look crystal clear:
Mr. Perfect-Baseball-Stud had been their favorite son all along.

If it were up to me, Bobblebutt would be on the first plane
to New Zealand or some other faraway place in the middle of
nowhere. The flight attendant would say, "Passengers, please fasten
your seat belts. We'll be serving six meals before reaching your final
destination. So enjoy your twenty-seven-hour flight."

Just the thought of being free of my bullying brother made me
feel better. Wishful thinking, I know. But if that were to happen,

I could invite Nutty over for dinner on Friday nights. Then we'd roast marshmallows in the fire pit outside and squish those blackened blobs between graham crackers. Yum.

Best of all, Nutty and I would have the whole family room to ourselves. We'd play video games until our battery warning lights flashed. We'd stay up all night, even after Dad and Mom went to bed, reading comic books with our flashlights. That would be great.

But for now, life sucks.

Your body hears everything your mind says. Stay positive.
— Naomi Judd —

4

Spider Legs

I tend to be a late-night binger, which probably isn't good for digestion. But pigging out on a bag of salty potato chips just before bedtime has become my nightly ritual. Eating in bed can be pretty messy, but I don't mind cleaning up afterwards. Plus, if crumbs fall between the sheets, Hershey and Dusty will lick 'em up—that's what dogs do.

Eating makes me happy. So if I'm having a good day, I usually eat something healthy, like a deli sandwich loaded with pastrami, tomatoes, lettuce, mustard, and pepperoncini. On lazy days—like during the weekends—I soften sourdough bread in the microwave and then smear my favorite apricot jam on top—amazing! On really bad days, I'll eat *anything* that looks good… even though my gut might suffer later because of my dumb dairy problem.

Since I'd had such an awful day, munching on a bag of chips didn't satisfy me. While everybody else was sleeping, I tiptoed downstairs to the kitchen for another snack.

The freezer was calling my name, so I opened it first. Hidden behind a bag of rock-solid veggies was a box of frozen dessert bars.

"Score!" I pumped my fist. "When did we get Double-Chocolatey Fudge Bars?" I read the ingredients on the side panel. Aw, crud. Chocolate ice cream dipped in milk chocolate. *That's* why they hid it from me. Maybe my stomach would feel okay if I just ate the chocolate outer layer. Then I could get rid of the rest of it… but I couldn't control the urge to eat the entire thing. Convincing myself it was okay to eat it took two seconds flat; removing the foil wrapper took another fifteen seconds; and forty-five seconds later, the whole ice-cream bar was gone—and I was *happy.*

Sometimes my body can process small amounts of dairy, as long as I take a digestion pill before eating anything with milk. But feeling nervous about being caught snacking at midnight made this little piggy forget to eat his chewable pill. Big mistake. And... for the next five hours, I became good friends with my toilet.

While lying on the bathroom floor at 4:00 a.m., feeling sorry for myself, I prayed for the willpower to step away from milk chocolate—or anything that would give me a stomachache. It wouldn't be easy, though, since I've always loved chocolate. I decided to take Nutty's advice and drink the *braaaain* juice.

I wasn't sure teaching my subconscious mind to dislike chocolate was even possible, but after a terrible night of stomach cramps and diarrhea, I was willing to try anything. So I imagined peeling back the foil of a chocolate-covered ice-cream bar and seeing a black, hairy tarantula wrapped all the way around it. I pictured the fanged spider slobbering all over my frozen dessert—that alone made me wanna puke.

Just the thought of eating Double-Chocolatey Fudge Bars makes me sick to my stomach—or maybe I'm feeling pukey because I ate the whole thing. Either way, it works! I've decided that I am never going to eat those ice cream bars again! Next time I'll have to try drinking some *braaaain* juice before I'm tempted to eat anything unhealthy.

Believe you can, and you're halfway there.
— Theodore Roosevelt —

5
Science Fair Trio

Usually Dad and Mom let me stay up until midnight on weekends as long as I read or do something constructive—like homework. *Boring*. But yesterday was Monday, and after that chocolate ice-cream bar disaster last night, I was *exhausted* at school.

During science class my tired eyes were glued shut for the first twenty minutes—not a good way to start the day.

"Does anybody have any toothpicks?" I said under my breath between yawns. "I need something to keep my eyelids open."

Amy Marie, who was seated right next to me, tossed two paper clips onto my desk. "Wanna use these?" She smiled and tipped the brim of her baseball cap, as if to say "you're welcome."

"Thanks," I whispered, trying not to lose class participation points.

Ames (that's Amy Marie's nickname) seems pretty cool. Last week Mr. Green, our science teacher, asked Nutty and me to be her dissection partners during the science lab. I really liked working with her because she wasn't squeamish about the formaldehyde solution. Other girls gagged when they smelled the slimy liquid used to preserve dead animals; Ames put her face right up to the pinned frogs, sliced 'em in half, poked at their guts—and smiled.

Mr. Green was the most popular teacher at Riverdale Middle School. Everybody knew that he drank lots of coffee to stay awake, because he was a science teacher by day and a rock 'n' roll musician by night. Rumor had it that he wore a band t-shirt underneath his dress shirt—but nobody knew for sure. He kept a coffee maker in the science lab next to our classroom, and sometimes he'd disappear for a few minutes and return with a steaming-hot mug of liquid energy.

"Class," said Mr. Green, "as you know, we'll be putting together our projects for the science fair. You'll need to do research, collect supplies, and decorate a poster board. If you haven't already, you'll also need to decide on a topic and choose partners. The sign-up sheet is on the door. You'll be working together in groups of two or three, and you'll be graded as a team."

Ames tossed another paper clip onto my desk and smiled. "Let's be partners! As long as it's something gross and messy, you can count me in."

She seemed a bit creepy, yet I kind of liked that about her. Ames always wore a baseball cap, with her blonde hair pulled forward in braids, and two-inch-high Skechers. Maybe she was trying to make up for being the shortest one in seventh grade. I'd seen her sitting by herself sometimes at lunch and wondered if she had any friends.

"Sorry," I said, "Nutty and I already signed up to be partners."

Nutty was sitting on the other side of the room, so he couldn't hear our conversation.

"But didn't you hear him?" Ames asked. "Mr. Green said we could work in teams of two or three. We could be a science fair trio!"

I didn't know what to say. "Um… " Maybe it wouldn't be such a bad idea. "Well, I don't see why not. But first let me ask Nutty."

"Great!" Ames gave me a thumb's up. She was acting as if I'd said yes… actually, I *wanted* to say yes. Half of me felt nervous, because I hadn't asked Nutty, but the other half was excited she wanted to be on our team. We'd had so much fun dissecting frogs last week, and I was really hoping that Nutty wouldn't mind.

"You'll be happy to know"—Mr. Green spoke in a loud voice, redirecting everyone's attention to the front of the class—"that one of the judges for this year's science fair will be a journalist from *River Valley Magazine*. She'll be choosing three student projects to be featured on the cover of the magazine, so your ideas could be showcased in next month's issue. Remember—creativity is important."

When the bell rang for lunch, Nutty said he'd meet me at the cafeteria. I waited until everybody had left the room except for Mr. Green and walked to the front of the class.

"Hi, Mr. Green."

"Hey, Louie. How are ya?"

"Fine, thanks. Um..." This was awkward. I should've planned what to say. "Would it be all right if Nutty and I do our science fair project on food allergies, because he's allergic to nuts and I can't eat dairy?"

"That sounds like an interesting topic."

"Really? Oh, thanks." My cheeks felt hot.

For the first time since school had started, I felt comfortable talking to Mr. Green. He had no idea how much I looked up to him as a role model.

"You're very welcome, Louie." He walked over to the white-board and grabbed an eraser.

"Thanks." I said, walking away.

"Oh, by the way," said Mr. Green, "I just talked to Amy Marie and added her to your group. You, Nutty, and Ames worked so well together dissecting frogs that I asked her to team up with you for the science fair. She didn't have a partner—hope you don't mind."

I felt like jumping up and down—not sure why, but my heart was definitely racing faster. "Yeah, sure. Ames is cool. I'll tell Nutty." I was relieved that Mr. Green had made the decision for us, because now Nutty couldn't get mad about having Ames on our team.

You have no idea how one conversation, one word of encouragement,
or one expression of love might change someone's life.
— Anonymous —

Ames

6

Puberty

I grabbed my backpack and beelined it to the cafeteria, where Nutty was waiting for me.

"Hey, dude," I climbed over the bench seat and sat across from him.

Nutty took a bite of his bologna sandwich and then looked at me strangely.

"What's that fuzzy thing crawling on your face?"

"What fuzzy thing?" I said, freaking out.

"It looks like a caterpillar," he said. "What are you gonna name it?" He laughed and pointed at my upper lip.

I had no idea what he was talking about. So I did what any seventh-grade boy would have done: I jumped up from the lunch table, swatted my face with both hands, and screamed.

Nutty laughed so hard that milk spewed from his nose and mouth. "Dude, I didn't mean a real caterpillar! I was talking about your new mustache!"

Eric Peevy and his friends—the hungry wolves—must've overheard us and, smelling weakness, decided to shred my self-esteem in front of the entire school. They rolled up tiny pieces of notebook paper, dribbled saliva onto each one, and then used plastic straws to fire slobbery spit wads at the back of my head while yelling, "Louie, do you also have hair growing on your chest?"

I wanted to shove those straws up their noses, but then they probably would've beaten me up after school. So instead I grabbed my backpack and lunch cooler, glared at Nutty, and sprinted toward the nearest exit.

I didn't realize that Eric had followed me until he knocked my lunch cooler to the ground. I stumbled and fell sideways—and landed on Ames, who was sitting alone at a table.

"*Ooof!* Sorry!" I scrambled to my feet, visions of a pressure-filled volcano exploding inside my head.

"That's okay," she said. We looked at each other for an awkward moment. She was obviously trying not to smile, and my face must've been beet red. Then I bolted out of there and didn't look back.

Angry and ashamed, I hid in the library until the end of lunch period. And since I'd forgotten to grab my cooler off the floor, I couldn't eat my lunch. "Now what?" I mumbled under my breath. "I guess I'll just have to starve."

Two things kept racing through my mind: First, Nutty was in the doghouse. He owed me an apology. Second, I couldn't stop thinking about Ames. She was the only person who didn't laugh at me, and it felt good—it felt really good...

Five foot two
with eyes of blue;
she's a tomboy through and through.
When she looked at me
all I could do
was wonder if she noticed me too.

Long, braided hair
pulled back from her face,
a gentle smile
that made my heart race.

What is this feeling?
I haven't a clue.
(What rhymes with clue? No idea—I'm not a poet.)
If I were a cow,
I would definitely... moo?

Now, more than ever, I wanted Ames to be my partner for the science fair. And as for Nutty, he definitely deserved the silent treatment.

I've learned that people will forget what you said, people will forget what you did, but people will never forget how you made them feel.
— *Maya Angelou* —

7

Buzz Off

When the final bell rang, I hurried over to the bike rack where Nutty and I usually meet after school. He was nowhere in sight. Good. I didn't want to see him anyway. I unchained my bike, strapped on my helmet, and took off down the road.

As I pedaled as fast as I could, the only thing on my mind was a three-letter word—nap. After that horrible night on the bathroom floor, I couldn't stop daydreaming about stretching out on the sofa, eating a bag of potato chips, and napping until dinnertime. Homework could wait until after I'd gotten some sleep.

When I pulled up to the house, Mom was standing outside the front door, talking with one of her fourth-grade students. The girl had just been dropped off for tutoring, so I didn't want to interrupt them. I waved to Mom, rode my bike to the side gate, and entered through the kitchen. Having strangers in the house always felt uncomfortable to me, but Mom was careful to keep the tutoring business separate from family time.

I grabbed a bag of chips and jogged into the family room. With a running start, I launched myself over the back of the sofa—like I'd done a million times before—and grabbed the remote control.

Hershey and Dusty barked at me like crazy, so I played tug-of-war with them until they pooped out—which doesn't take long for our shih-tzus.

Hershey's white, fluffy tail and jiggly butt looked as cute as ever. He pawed at the sofa, so I plopped him on the seat next to me, where he snuggled up against my leg—and started growling at Dusty, who had jumped on the couch to join us. "Deal with it,

Mr. Jealous," I said to Hershey before I buried my face in Dusty's chest and said, "You're so darn cute and tiny!" He cooed like a songbird and licked my hand. Then both of them curled up next to my leg and fell asleep.

After playing video games for about fifteen minutes, I no longer felt sleepy, so I decided to skip the nap and get my homework done. Both doggies were still fast asleep, so I carefully snuck past them and grabbed my backpack from the kitchen. But when I returned, both pups had already left the room.

Something didn't feel right. I heard a strange noise and then something flew by my face. I glanced around the room... *oh my gosh*. I didn't like bothering Mom while she was tutoring, but this was important.

"Um—Mom, may I talk to you for a minute?"

"Sure," She excused herself from her student and met me in the hallway. "Is everything okay?"

"We have a problem! I was about to do my homework in the family room when I heard a buzzing sound. Something pretty big flew by the TV, and then another one flew right by my face. When I looked at the sliding glass door, which was open, there were a bunch of bees on the screen. Inside the house."

"*What?*" Her eyes got really big.

"Yeah," I said. "So I closed the glass door really fast. The bees are trapped, but they're really angry."

"You did the right thing, Louie." She sounded worried.

"Thanks. But I'm freaking out, because I still hear a lot of buzzing in there."

We tiptoed down the hallway and stared into the family room. Both of us stood there without moving.

"Listen," she said.

I heard a faint buzzing sound over by the fireplace and said, "Do you hear them?"

"Shhh. Let's listen closely, to find out if many of them are in the house."

I whispered, "I'll check out back, Mom."

"Sounds good. Be careful, Louie."

Mom's tutoring session had just ended, so she brought her student outside to get picked up by her parents. After they drove away, Mom canceled the rest of her appointments for the day, since she didn't want a swarm of bees to sting anybody. Then she called a beekeeper.

I looked around for any sign of bees, which seemed dangerous and risky, but I wanted to be brave since Mom needed my help. So I said a quick prayer and forged ahead, imagining that I'd strapped on God's protective shield of courage, something Pastor Rusty talked about a few weeks ago at church. I walked into the backyard and looked up at the chimney—where thousands of swarming bees were flying overhead! And then I saw hundreds of bees *inside* the house, buzzing behind the curtain in the family room. "Oh my gosh! They're coming in through the fireplace!" I ran inside to tell Mom.

We used plastic trash bags and masking tape to seal off the doorway into the family room; that way bees wouldn't escape into the rest of the house. Since the humming sound was frazzling my nerves, Mom and I stood outside and waited for the beekeeper to arrive. He showed up wearing a white beekeeper's suit with white gloves and a white hat that covered his entire face—crazy! He was able to find a new home for all the little buzzers—although I was sure I'd be flicking imaginary bees away from my body for days.

Later that night, Dad used more trash bags and masking tape to cover the fireplace so stragglers wouldn't buzz into the house. Our bee-free home was back to normal, and it was nice to hang out in the family room again.

Kent and I agreed to watch TV together—as long as we didn't talk. So we sat on the sofa and watched an episode of *Commander Courageous*. Even though my brother annoyed me, sitting in silence was better than being alone—especially since I was giving Nutty the silent treatment.

———— ⌒⌒ ————

That night, I had a terrifying nightmare. I will never look at honey bees the same again. I dreamed that I was a worker bee with beautiful wings, and I loved building wax chambers for our honeycomb. Thousands of my friends were building a hive; we chewed and softened the wax and were happy to have found a new home inside of a chimney. Then a giant white creature destroyed our colony by throwing smoke bombs at us. I woke up sweating and feeling sad about losing all of my bee friends—and also my *best* friend.

For the rest of the night, I lay awake thinking about the importance of bees and wondering how our science fair project could make a difference. What if we use honey instead of sugar for a recipe? It would be much healthier, and everybody would be able to appreciate the hard work that bees put into making honey.

Still, it felt like a part of me was missing because I couldn't share my idea with Nutty. Even though I was still mad at him about the caterpillar joke, I needed to get over it. We were more like brothers than friends, and since it felt like I'd already lost Kent, I didn't want to lose Nutty too. That's why I decided to take the high road and forgive him—as long as he promised not to do it again. Now it was just a matter of telling Nutty.

If the bee disappeared off the face of the earth,
man would only have four years left to live.
— *Maurice Maeterlinck, The Life of the Bee* —

8

Eat the Frog

Today I decided to eat the frog. Well, not literally. Who wants to put a slimy amphibian into their mouth? It's just something that people say when they decide to do the most uncomfortable thing *first*, before tackling anything else. So the big, wart-covered frog that I needed to "eat" was telling Nutty that he shouldn't have embarrassed me in front of everybody at school.

Running from Eric Peevy's spitballs was no fun. But it was nothing compared to getting teased by my best friend about having a mustache—puberty of all things!

I didn't want to hold a grudge against Nutty, so right before first period we had a heated argument by the lockers about my 'mustache' and how he embarrassed me in the cafeteria. He eventually gave in and apologized, and I agreed to let it go and move on.

After school, we hopped on our bikes and rode to Fresh Market since we were going to make Sunbutter Chocolate Bars for the church bake sale. As we coasted downhill—laughing and riding with our hands in the air—it dawned on me that I still hadn't mentioned anything to him about Ames joining our science fair team. So after we locked our bikes in front of the store, I told him what Mr. Green said on Monday, and Nutty was totally fine with it—phew! I worried for nothing.

"So what are we gonna buy?" Nutty asked as we walked into the store together.

"I wrote down a list of ingredients," I said, pulling a wrinkled piece of paper out of my pocket. "We'll need three cups of creamy sunbutter, two cups of gluten-free graham cracker crumbs, two cups of powdered sugar, two cups of rice flour, one cup of organic buttery spread, one bag of semisweet dairy-free chocolate chips, and honey to drizzle over the cookies."

"That sounds expensive!" Nutty said.

"No, it'll be fine," I told him. "My mom gave me forty bucks. She said we should just keep track of the money we spend and then subtract it from the church donation."

"Got it!" Nutty smiled and rubbed his hands together. "So if we sell twenty-four Sunbutter Chocolate Bars for two fifty per piece, we would earn…" He closed his eyes and calculated the equation in his head. "Dude, that's sixty bucks!"

"Sixty bucks!" I was excited. "Are you serious?"

"Yeah! Do the math."

$2.50 x 24 = $60.00

He's right!

We danced like a couple of crazed monkeys and laughed until our stomachs hurt.

"All right! Let's get this party started," I said.

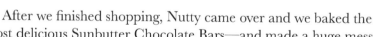

After we finished shopping, Nutty came over and we baked the most delicious Sunbutter Chocolate Bars—and made a huge mess in the kitchen. The bake sale was the next day, so Mom offered to drop off our desserts at the church in the morning.

Just knowing that Nutty and I were best friends again made everything a million times better. Being angry—even just for a day—seemed like such a waste of energy. And the time apart made me appreciate him more—like a brother. It reminded me of how we'd always been there for each other—*no matter what.*

Eat a live frog first thing in the morning and nothing worse will happen to you the rest of the day.
— Mark Twain —

Nutty

9

Those Blasted Peanuts

Nutty is deathly allergic to peanuts, so worrying about food is part of his DNA. His parents have serious food allergies too, so they're three times as paranoid about eating anything that isn't homemade.

I remember sitting in the cafeteria with Nutty when we were in fifth grade. Vidal, a new kid, sat at our table and started eating a peanut butter and jelly sandwich. Nutty looked at him with disgust and said, "Could you please not eat peanuts around me, dude?"

Vidal, who seemed nice enough, asked, "Why not?"

Nutty said, "Because I'm allergic to peanuts, dingdong," almost as if the new kid should've known.

"Oh," said Vidal, who ignored Nutty and kept chewing his sandwich. "What happens if you eat one?"

"I don't know," Nutty said sarcastically, "Maybe I'd puke on your lunch and then morph into a peanut zombie." He stood up, groaned with outstretched arms, and walked toward Vidal with jerking movements. Vidal must've not appreciated Nutty's snide humor, because he packed up his lunch, and left the table.

Even though Nutty can be harsh to people, I've learned to keep my mouth shut. Mom has always said, "You need to give him grace, Louie. You can't truly understand someone until you've walked a mile in his shoes."

I can totally relate to Nutty's frustration, since both of us have had food issues since birth. But his peanut allergy can be life-threatening, so when people don't consider that, he blows a gasket!

31

A few weeks ago, our families got together after church for a potluck, which was set up in the rec room. Rows of folding chairs and tables lined the room, piled high with delicious-looking food. Nutty raised an eyebrow and motioned for me to follow him. We broke away from the others and headed toward the veggie table.

When we finally made our way to the front of the line, Nutty reached over the table and grabbed a celery stick. Just before taking a bite, he looked down and noticed a glass bowl next to the veggie tray; it was overflowing with peanut butter, and several stalks of celery had been stuck in it as decoration. Nutty *froze*—and then, without warning, hurled his celery stick across the room, where it landed in a bowl of chocolate pudding.

He yelled out, "Really? Who put PEANUT BUTTER next to the celery sticks? I thought that I could eat SOMETHING here, but now I can't eat ANYTHING!"

Most of the adults standing near him looked confused as Nutty stormed out of the rec room and disappeared into the church hallway.

I followed him to the bathroom. "Nutty, are you okay?"

A whimpering voice came from the back stall. "No. This party's stupid. The food's stupid. Everybody who brought food is stupid."

"I know, dude."

"Why aren't people more considerate?" He sniffled. "And who brought *peanut butter* with celery sticks? It was the *one thing* I could've eaten besides the *dumb* snack bar my mom brought, and now there's nothing for me."

I felt bad for him. "Hey, bro," I said, "I'm really sorry. And if it makes you feel any better, I'm not gonna eat any of that stupid food either."

I sat on the bathroom floor next to the sink, and he stayed inside the stall. There we were, hanging out in the church bathroom, not saying a word for ten minutes, but I wanted him to know he wasn't alone. When our parents came looking for us, Nutty walked out of the stall with swollen eyes and gave me a fist bump.

Peanuts have been Nutty's archnemesis since he was two years old. It all started on Halloween night, when he ate his first chocolate-covered peanut. Even though I was young, I still have vivid memories from that day—of him coughing and vomiting all over the floor... of the huge rash covering his chest and back. I'll never forget it. His parents had to rush their purple dinosaur to the hospital, where two nurses gave him epinephrine shots—one in each thigh—and saved his life.

Fast forward to today. Nutty always carries epinephrine shots in his backpack just in case he accidentally eats something with peanuts. Even though he's embarrassed to tell people about it, I actually think it's kind of cool. And who knows? Maybe he'll become an allergy doctor someday and save other people's lives.

Peanut allergy symptoms can be life-threatening (anaphylaxis).
For some people... even tiny amounts of peanuts
can cause a serious reaction.
— MayoClinic.org —

10
Gooey Chocolate Bars

The day after our trip to Fresh Market, I was in the best mood. Nutty and I were on speaking terms, and life was good. Plus, I got an A on my math test!

I was playing video games on the sofa after school when Mom walked into the kitchen from the garage, carrying bags of groceries.

"Hey, Louie!"

"Hi, Mom." I gave her a quick wave and then turned back to the TV. I probably should've offered to help, but I was just about to level up in my game.

"Hey, would you and Nutty like to come with me to a cooking party on Saturday?"

I was lost in the game. "A cooking party? Um… sure. But we don't really know how to cook."

Mom walked over to me and kissed my cheek. "That's exactly why you two should tag along," she said. "I ran into Ms. Cynthia at the market, and she invited us to the party. There should be lots of yummy food to taste, and you two might get inspired—I know how much you like baking desserts."

I paused the video game and turned toward her. "But Nutty won't go since he won't be able to eat anything."

"Just tell him I'll make something special for *both* of you to eat."

"Really? Okay!" It actually did sound like fun.

Mom pulled up a chair next to me. "Louie, I hope you don't mind—I told Ms. Cynthia about your lactose intolerance."

What? *Great.* Why did Mom have to tell a lady from church—or anybody—about my personal gut issues? Isn't there a law against that? She shouldn't be telling people about my dairy problem and diarrhea, especially when they're shopping for food—yuck.

"Well, what did she say?" I asked.

"We can bring our own food to the party. She said that would be fine."

"*No,*" I was getting irritated. "I mean what did she say about my *private* health issue?"

Mom must've gotten the message, because she tried to change the subject instead of answering my question. She hugged me and said, "Louie, Ms. Cynthia loved the Sunbutter Chocolate Bars that you and Nutty made for the church bake sale. She wants the recipe."

That was a shocker. "Really?"

"Yup."

"But we changed the recipe."

"I know," Mom said with a big smile. "And everybody loved *your* recipe!"

I turned off my video game and tossed the remote control onto the table. I wanted to process what she was saying.

"When you guys replaced white flour with sweet rice flour, the mixture became delicious and gooey. Your treats probably tasted *better* than the original recipe."

"You think so?" I didn't feel that confident about our baking skills—the kitchen had looked like a tornado hit it after Nutty and I made the Sunbutter Chocolate Bars.

"Absolutely!" Mom said with a high five. "Hey, since you've changed the ingredients, why don't you guys change the name to *Gooey* Chocolate Bars? With a name like that, people would *definitely* buy them."

"Gooey Chocolate Bars—I like it!"

Mom laughed. "The next time you see Nutty, please show him this catalog." She handed me a small booklet. "Or, better yet, just invite him to Ms. Cynthia's cooking party. It's this Saturday at two o'clock. And we can pick him up."

All this talk about cooking got me excited for our science fair project. "Cool. Thanks, Mom!"

"Anytime, buddy." She stood up and pointed toward the kitchen. "That could be your test kitchen. You guys could do experiments with different desserts, as long as you have a plan."

"What do you mean?"

"Just find one or two dessert recipes that both of you like. If any of them include nuts or dairy, then just substitute ingredients—like you did with the sweet rice flour. If you create nut-free, dairy-free dessert recipes of your own, people will want to buy them."

My brain was reeling with ideas. I couldn't wait to tell Nutty.

"You guys could even start a business, Louie!" She high fived me again. "Dad, Kent, and I could be your first customers. You could even sell them to the baseball team families."

"Oh my gosh! That would be awesome! Thanks, Mom."

I ran upstairs, grabbed my phone, and called Nutty. He didn't answer, so I sent him a text: "Hey, man. What are you doing on Saturday? There's something I need to tell you!"

*People with lactose intolerance are unable to fully digest
the sugar (lactose) in milk. As a result, they have diarrhea,
gas and bloating after eating or drinking dairy products.*
— Mayo Clinic.org —

11

Shield of Courage

The next morning at school, I met up with Nutty at his locker.

"Hey, man," he said. "What was up with your text last night?"

I was dying to tell him about Mom's cooking business idea, but the first period bell was about to ring. "Can I tell you at lunch? Otherwise, we'll be late to class."

"Sure. No problem." Nutty slammed his locker door, and we ran to language arts.

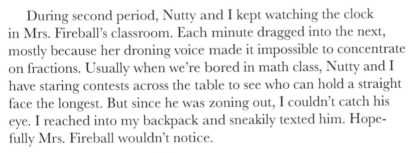

During second period, Nutty and I kept watching the clock in Mrs. Fireball's classroom. Each minute dragged into the next, mostly because her droning voice made it impossible to concentrate on fractions. Usually when we're bored in math class, Nutty and I have staring contests across the table to see who can hold a straight face the longest. But since he was zoning out, I couldn't catch his eye. I reached into my backpack and sneakily texted him. Hopefully Mrs. Fireball wouldn't notice.

ME: Wake up, dude! lol

Nutty's phone vibrated in his front pocket, startling him from a daze. I watched as he glanced around and then slipped his phone underneath the table.

NUTTY: Hey. We're not supposed to be texting. lol

ME: I know! But I can't wait to tell you about our business. Cha-ching!

NUTTY: I'm still half asleep, man. I've got serious brain fog.

ME: Bro, we can make a ton of $$$! Meet me after class, okay?

NUTTY: What are you talking about?

ME: Later.

I put my phone away so Mrs. Fireball wouldn't catch me texting.

Nutty looked at me across the table, raised his eyebrows, and shook with silent laughter. "Why do we have to learn this stuff anyway?" he whispered, pointing toward the white board in front of the classroom.

"I know," I mouthed, rolling my eyes.

Mrs. Fireball's suddenly shrill voice interrupted our conversation. "Nathan and Louie! Is there something that you two would like to share with the rest of the class?"

Oops! *Busted.*

"Yes, ma'am," said Nutty, sitting up quickly in his chair. He looked like he was trying to control his laughter. "We're just not sure how to use these fractions in everyday life."

"Really?" she said sarcastically. "Well, do you know how to cook?"

"A little bit."

"Good." She folded her long, stick-like arms. "Do you use measuring cups?"

"Sometimes."

"So, do you think that measuring cups might have something to do with fractions?"

Nutty shrugged. "Maybe?"

Everybody laughed, except for Nutty and me. I slumped down lower into my seat, hoping Mrs. Fireball wouldn't put the spotlight on me next.

She walked toward Nutty and said, "Using measuring cups is the best way to combine ingredients when baking or cooking. For example, if you're doubling a cake recipe that calls for $1\frac{1}{2}$ cups of flour, then you'd add $1\frac{1}{2}$ cups plus $1\frac{1}{2}$ cups, which equals 3 cups."

All eyes were on Nutty, and he was starting to fall apart under the pressure.

Mrs. Fireball turned her tall, lanky body toward the rest of the class. "Who would like to give Nutty another example of how to use fractions while cooking?" A few kids raised their hands, but she ignored them and slowly walked in my direction with a frown on her face. "Louie, how about you?"

Even though I was cringing inside, I decided not to let Mrs. Fireball shake me. I thought about what Mom said the other morning—"pray for strength"—so I decided to give it a whirl. I imagined I was a thick-skinned black rhino, shielding myself from the scorching flames spewing from Mrs. Fireball's mouth.

"God will protect me," I mumbled under my breath.

"Excuse me?" said Mrs. Fireball.

I gathered my confidence and said, "Actually, I'm thinking about becoming a chef, so I can definitely give you an example."

The class roared with laughter, and even Mrs. Fireball's lips twitched. Surprisingly, I didn't get upset. The prayer must've helped. It was the most freeing feeling, knowing that God had given me courage to stand tall.

"I wasn't kidding. I really do love to cook," I said. "In fact, I'm thinking about making something for the science fair."

Nutty's jaw dropped. He'd never heard me say anything about becoming a chef, since I hadn't had a chance to tell him about our new business.

Mrs. Fireball smirked. "And what exactly are you planning to cook, Chef Pickle?"

"Allergy-friendly desserts," I said.

"Really?" said Mrs. Fireball, eyebrows raised. "Well, good for you, Louie. Now please explain to the class how you'll use fractions to make your allergy-friendly desserts."

I felt thick rhino skin growing over my chest and back. In a confident voice that surprised even me, I said, "After you get all of the ingredients together, you follow the recipe directions. So if you need 1½ cups of water, 3¼ cups of flour, and 2 cups of sugar, just mix them together. And if you want to double the recipe, multiply everything by 2."

She seemed genuinely impressed. "Very nice, Louie."

But I wasn't done yet. "So $1\frac{1}{2}$ cups of water multiplied by 2 equals 3 cups of water."

"That's correct, Mr. Pickle."

"And $3\frac{1}{4}$ cups of flour times 2 equals $6\frac{2}{4}$ cups of flour, which is the same as $6\frac{1}{2}$ cups of flour."

"Impressive," she said.

"And of course 2 times 2 equals 4 cups of sugar. That's easy."

Nutty flashed me a huge grin. And some of the kids in the class actually clapped! I sat back in my chair and relished the moment. For the first time, I actually felt like one of the smart kids in Mrs. Fireball's class.

Courage doesn't mean you don't get afraid.
Courage means you don't let fear stop you.
— Bethany Hamilton —

12

Am I Invisible?

Nutty had to stay after math class to complete a make-up test, so I was walking to my locker alone when somebody came up from behind me and tapped my shoulder. It was Eric Peevy and his annoying friends.

"Hey, Louie," said Eric. "That was really cool what you did back there in math class." Then he stepped in front of me and said, "I guess you're not as dumb as you look."

I didn't think it was a compliment but said, "Um… thanks." Did I just thank him for calling me dumb?

Eric shook his head with disgust, rolled his eyes, and took a step closer to me. He was in my personal space—so close that I could smell peanut butter on his breath.

"Maybe you should've learned how to read, too," he said, "instead of *re-re-reading* like a first grader." He laughed loudly.

Eric's friends, Jack and Ryan, copied their leader. "Yeah, *re-re-reading* like a first grader!"

Then the leader and his pack of wolves circled around me. Jack yanked my backpack off my shoulders and threw it on the ground. Ryan stomped on my shoe, leaving a black mark across the toe. And Eric, the alpha wolf—I imagined a thick coat of grayish-black hair growing beneath his shirt—stuck his finger in my face and snarled, "Chef Pickle, you'd better not make that *stupid* dessert for the science fair, or I'll make sure you're the laughing stock of seventh grade."

My stomach tightened into a knot.

"And if you *do* make it," he said, "then it'd better not taste good." He punched his left fist into his right hand. "Or else your face will feel like *this*." He pulled back his clenched fist and released a spring-loaded punch into my right shoulder. "Because *I'm* gonna win first prize!" Then he and his friends rushed off to their classrooms.

I stood in the hallway, frozen, holding my shoulder and choking back tears. Pain radiated down my right arm—it felt like I'd been hit with a sledgehammer.

Other kids walked right by me. Nobody offered to help or asked if I was okay. A few told me to move out of their way—their voices sounded distant, like echoes from a black hole in another galaxy.

Strangely, I couldn't move my feet. I could barely blink my eyes. I almost forgot how to breathe. Finally, as if released from a spell, I took a gasping breath and then exhaled. Back to reality. Except, for the first time in my life, I felt *invisible*.

The second bell had already rung, and other than me, nobody was in the hallway. I was alone. I picked up my backpack and went to the closest bathroom. Getting punched seemed like a perfectly legit reason to ditch class and hide in a bathroom stall.

I stood on a toilet seat and squatted down. That way nobody would see my feet, and bathroom monitors couldn't find me. If any kids came into the bathroom and noticed my stall door was locked, they'd just use a different one.

All I could think about was how much I needed my best friend. Why was he sitting in some dumb class when I needed him the most? When he was hiding in the bathroom stall at church, I was there for him. Did Nutty—or anybody else, for that matter—really care about me?

The thought of telling Dad and Mom about being bullied stressed me out to the max. What if Bobblebutt found out and teased me about it? The last thing I needed was another verbal attack from *him*. Just thinking about it made my heart race, so I tried to relax by closing my eyes—but then it felt like I was swimming in a sea of darkness. I needed help. I wanted to vent about what had just happened, but nobody was around, so I decided to pour my heart out to God.

Hey, God, it's Louie.
Could you please help me?
I'm in misery and hurting badly.

Will anybody stop to look for me,
while I'm hiding out and feeling lonely?
Probably not. Maybe. Eventually.

If I could have one wish it would be
to throw every bully onto a ship at sea;
I'd send them far, far away from me.
That alone would set me free.

Look, I don't want to be mean;
I'm just hoping those guys will see
that I'm not stupid, like it might seem.
I can read, just not with lightning speed.

So why did Eric have to punch me?
He should be punished; don't you agree?
I'm struggling; please help me to breathe.

Maybe you're busy creating galaxies,
But hopefully you'll notice me.
At least send your angel army
to deliver a swarm of angry bees
to repay Eric and his two cronies
for the pain they've caused me.

And then, for the grand finale,
help us to bake for the winning team.
Please help Nutty, Ames, and me
to earn a trophy for the magazine.
We'll do our very best to achieve.
And when we win first place, you'll see,
Eric's fist won't get the best of me.

When bad things happened to me in the past, I usually broke into a million pieces and went into hiding for days. Nutty would wonder why I wasn't returning texts, and Dad and Mom would chalk it up to pre-teen hormones, but life still continued as always. Nothing had ever been done to fix the problem. But becoming a human punching bag was definitely a wakeup call. The ugly truth was that being bullied at home and at school was doubly depressing.

I remembered Pastor Rusty's message at church on Sunday. Maybe I'm living in the darkroom of my life, and God's trying to develop me into a stronger person—I just need to ask Him for help. But sometimes I have a hard time believing that God's really listening to me. I mean, there are a gazillion other people out there with more urgent prayers—so why would He care about *mine?* And how does He even have time for me? I guess that's where I need to grow the most. Pastor Rusty said I just need to believe—that I don't need to know everything *about* the faith to have faith; it'll come in time.

So right there, hiding in the bathroom and crouched on a toilet seat, I decided to walk in faith and follow God's lead. I decided that a peaceful life at home and school was possible. I decided to brush off my shoulder pain and not let Eric's iron fist change my attitude. I decided to rise above my anger and ask for God's strength instead of disappearing into the dark corners of my mind. I knew that it wasn't going to be easy and that it would take time for the bullying to end, but I was willing to do my part by praying and asking for help.

And I wasn't going to let any of this dampen my excitement about our dessert business—or keep us from winning that science fair contest.

When the bell rang after second period, I left the bathroom and headed to my locker.

Nutty ran toward me with a big smile on his face. "Hey, dude. Where've you been? That make-up test was a breeze!" He dropped his backpack on the ground, unzipped the front cover, and started hunting for a granola bar.

Little did he know, just being with him made me feel like myself again—*visible.* I didn't want to ruin Nutty's great mood, so I chose not to tell him yet about getting punched or hiding in the bathroom.

We walked to science class together, and I waved the cooking party booklet in front of his face. "Check it out!" I was surprised by my enthusiasm, considering the recent events and my throbbing shoulder.

"What is it?" Nutty asked.

"We're going to a party!"

"What? What do you mean?" He laughed and grabbed the booklet from my hand.

"My mom's friend loved the dessert we baked—"

"Oh yeah, bro! You really surprised everybody in math class with those fractions!" He pushed my right shoulder jokingly.

I pulled back quickly and said, "Don't!"

Nutty frowned and shook his head. "Whatever, man."

"Remember those Sunbutter Chocolate Bars we made for the church bake sale?" I said, trying to change the subject.

He nodded, still chewing his granola bar.

"My mom thinks we should sell them."

Nutty started flipping through the cooking catalog. "I'm totally confused. How can we sell anything if we have nothing to sell? These are pots and pans."

"Dude, that's the catalog for the cooking party. *We'll* be selling our Gooey Chocolate Bars—not those things."

"Gooey Chocolate Bars?"

I realized that there was so much more I needed to tell him. "Just come with me tomorrow to the cooking party, all right? I'll explain everything then. But for now, text me a list of your favorite desserts. We'll need to come up with new recipe ideas for our business."

"But—"

"We should also decide which new video games and comic books to buy, because we'll be swimming in *money!*"

That got his attention. "*Money?*" Nutty stepped forward, eyes widening. "Just by selling desserts?"

"Yup." I gave him a fist bump and we walked into Mr. Green's science lab, where we did our best to concentrate on the life cycle of plants.

But during those forty minutes of class, my mind wandered. I imagined pushing a shopping cart through Game Mart and tossing handfuls of video games into the basket without worrying about money. Judging by Nutty's expression, I figured his wheels were spinning, too. His mind was probably ten thousand miles away—thinking about buying a ticket to Comic-Con, adding hundreds of comic books to his collection, and feeling the crisp, new pages of *Commander Courageous's* up-and-coming edition *Fear Not!*

We had our work cut out for us, though. We couldn't let day-dreaming about having a successful dessert business distract us from our schoolwork, because our parents would only allow us to do it if we kept up our grades. So Nutty and I would have to make a pact to work even harder on homework every day. Our future depended on it.

The Lord is my strength and my shield;
my heart trusts in him, and he helps me.
— Psalm 28:7 (NIV) —

13

Facing My Fear

After that crazy day at school, I couldn't wait to go home and hide in my bedroom. It felt good to be in a safe place, to know that Eric Peevy couldn't hurt me. Inside the four walls of my room, I could control everything: music, lighting, snacks, doing homework or not doing homework, cleaning my room or leaving it a mess. But most important, I couldn't be bullied by Eric inside my own house.

Standing in front of my full-length mirror, I stared at my reflection, studying my hair, face, body, and feet. What was it about me that made Eric and his friends hate me so much? What did I do to deserve getting punched in the shoulder? Maybe Eric felt threatened by my science fair project idea because he thought it would be better than his. Or maybe he just found my reading problem annoying.

My arm and chest were aching, so I took off my shirt and checked out the damage. A purplish-red bruise had spread across my shoulder and was sore to the touch. I thought about getting an ice pack from the freezer but decided it was too risky. Dad, Mom, or Kent might see me with it and start asking questions, which was the *last* thing I needed.

But... maybe I *should* tell them what happened at school. Weren't people supposed to share things with their families? Only, I didn't want to concern Dad or Mom because their lives were already too stressful. And I definitely didn't want Kent to find out, because he'd tell me that I was stupid for not defending myself instead of offering to help like a normal brother. I was still lost in thought when Mom called up the stairs.

"Louie, come on down for dinner!"

My stomach was growling, so I raced downstairs to set the table.

"What are we eating?" I asked.

"Your favorite!" Mom had become a pro at whipping up great-tasting recipes, even with just a few ingredients. Her gluten-free spaghetti noodles with tomato sauce and a side of green beans was my all-time favorite meal.

"You made spaghetti? Awesome!" It had been weeks since we'd had spaghetti, so I was extra excited.

"Thank you for always loving my cooking, Louie!" She kissed my cheek. "By the way, Kent's still at baseball practice. So he won't be eating with us tonight."

Big-Burly-Bruiser-Bro wasn't gonna eat dinner with us? Dinnertime was actually going to be peaceful? Yes!

"How was school today?" Mom asked as she scooped steaming-hot noodles covered with red tomato sauce onto three plates.

"It was okay." That's the only thing I could think to say.

"Just okay?"

I didn't feel like answering, so I didn't say a word—hoping that she'd drop it.

Just then, Dad walked into the kitchen and sat down with us at the table—a perfect distraction—and we all began to devour the delicious meal. Even Hershey and Dusty were spoiled. When they begged for green beans, Mom mixed some with their food.

Just as I was standing up to clear my plate from the table, Mom dropped *the bomb*.

"So, Louie, I got a phone call today from the principal at your school."

Dad looked over the rim of his glasses and stared at me with disappointment. Well, so much for a perfectly peaceful dinner. My heart was beating so fast that blood was gushing through my veins at supersonic speed.

"Mr. McCracken left a voicemail message about you missing class today," she said.

Great. I'm literally gonna be grounded for *life*.

"After you listen to this message," she said, "please explain to us what happened at school."

Mom turned up the volume on her phone, and I heard Mr. McCracken's voice say, "Hi, Mrs. Pickle. This is Robert McCracken, principal at Riverdale Middle School. I'm not sure if you're aware, but Louie wasn't in his third-period class today. I spoke with Mrs. Fireball, who said that he was in her second-period math class. Yet, for whatever reason, he chose to skip out on Spanish class. We don't look favorably upon that type of behavior, mainly because of safety issues. So if you could please speak with him about it and get back to me, I would appreciate it. Thank you, Mrs. Pickle."

Every part of my body felt numb, and I forgot to breathe. All I wanted to do was run to my bedroom and sleep. Maybe if I slept for a week, all of the shame, embarrassment, and pain would disappear—and then I wouldn't have to answer to anybody.

Dad cleared his throat and crossed his arms. "What do you have to say about that, Louie?"

This was, by far, the worst day ever. But despite my panic, a four-letter word kept running through my mind—pray.

God, will you lend an ear?
Do you think that I should say
Anything about being bullied today?
Dad might ground me either way.

God, will you help me here?
Please show me the way
To make my stress go away.
Can you erase this terrible day?

God, how should I face my fear?
Maybe if I look into their eyes and say,
"I need your help, Dad and Mom, okay?
'Cause I'm tired of being Eric's prey."

God, will you make it clear?
Maybe they won't believe a word I say,
But I'm hoping that you can find a way
To show them that I'm not okay.

After slowly breathing through that prayer, I sat up in my seat and looked straight into Dad's eyes. At that moment, I realized it didn't matter what Dad or Mom had to say, because God had been with me all along. I felt strangely calm. Telling them what happened at school wasn't going to make Eric disappear, but at least it would help them understand my anxiety and hopefully help me through it. And since Kent wasn't home, it was a perfect time to tell them.

When God pushes you to the edge of difficulty, trust him fully
because two things can happen; either he'll catch you
when you fall or he'll teach you how to fly.
— Anonymous —

14

The Storm

"I was bullied today."

There. I said it. And I was proud of myself for not backing down.

Dad and Mom looked at each other and didn't say a word.

"A group of guys ganged up on me near my locker," I said nervously.

Mom gasped. "What!"

"They threw my backpack on the ground and made fun of me because of the way I read—because of my dyslexia. Then one of them punched me really hard on my shoulder. It hurt a *lot*, and I was really upset, so I hid in the bathroom."

The room was silent. Nobody said a word. Then Dad leaned forward and looked straight into my eyes.

"Louie," he said. "You were punched by a boy at school? Who did that to you?" He sounded more concerned than angry, which was a relief.

"Eric Peevy. He told me that I'd better not win the science fair contest or else—and then he hit me."

Mom's eyes filled with tears. She reached out and touched my hand. "Louie... I'm sorry."

Just seeing how much they cared made me feel better.

"Where did he punch you?" Dad asked.

Slowly, I lifted my shirt and showed them my right shoulder, which had started to swell. The bruise was the size of Eric's big fist, and his knuckles were imprinted on my skin.

Dad was *livid*. His face turned as reddish-purple as my bruise.

"Who the *bloody heck* is Eric Peevy? I want to speak with his parents!"

By then, Mom was sobbing—although I could tell she was trying to hold it together. She stood up and hugged me from behind the chair and then walked to the freezer and grabbed an ice pack.

"Here, my love," she said, "put this on your shoulder."

It was too cold to put directly on my skin, so I grabbed the ice pack and placed it on top of my shirt.

Dad stood up and paced back and forth.

"What kind of school is this?" he said. "Our son was bullied and punched, yet the principal didn't even know about it!"

Mom sat down next to me and put a comforting hand on my good shoulder. "Louie, please tell us exactly what happened."

So for the next five minutes, I told them everything, including how Eric and his friends had always bullied Nutty and me at school. Dad and Mom listened, and I didn't feel invisible.

When I was finished, Dad sat down across from me and asked, "Louie, why didn't you tell us before that Eric and his friends were bullying you?"

Really? Why didn't I tell him? Dad always laughed whenever Kent teased me at home, so why would I think he'd care about some bullies teasing me at school? But since he'd asked, maybe it was a good time to *finally* talk about it.

I thought about my prayer, took a deep breath, and said, "I'm glad you asked, Dad."

A bright flash of lightning lit up the room, followed by a loud crash of thunder. It had been drizzling all day, but I was startled by the sudden downpour. The three of us stood up and looked out the kitchen window. The rain was coming down in buckets, soaking the backyard.

"That's quite a storm. I wonder if it's going to hail," Dad said.

He closed the kitchen window and led us back to the table.

I smiled. God must've known that we needed a mini distraction to get us through this uncomfortable conversation.

"Let's get back to my question," Dad said. "Louie, is there a reason why you didn't tell us that Eric and his friends were bullying you at school?"

"Um," I said. "Honestly? I was afraid to tell you."

Mom frowned but didn't say anything.

"Afraid?" Dad asked, looking confused.

"Yes."

"Why were you afraid?"

"Because"—I swallowed a lump in my throat—"whenever Kent makes fun of me, you never really do anything about it. And you always think it's funny… but it's *not*."

Mom's mouth dropped open, and she covered it with both hands.

I said a quick prayer—*Lord, give me the right words to say.*

"I've lived with Kent's bullying my entire life, and you've never really done anything to stop him."

Dad stared at me with a blank expression on his face.

Then he said, "Has Kent ever hit you?"

"No," I said, rubbing the edge of the table nervously.

"Then why would you say that he's been bullying you?"

There was no turning back now.

"Well… he's been mean to me since birth," I said.

Dad scowled. "You're exaggerating."

"No, I'm not." I needed to be respectful—but direct. "Every memory that I have of Kent is *terrible*. And whenever we have dinner, he always finds something negative to say about me."

"Like what?"

I sighed. "Like the never-ending nose jokes. And lately he's been teasing me about how it whistles."

Dad laughed and shook his head.

My cheeks burned. It took every ounce of courage to say, "See? That's what I'm talking about, Dad. You're laughing, too."

"But it's funny, Louie. So your nose whistles, big deal. Stop being so sensitive. Your brother's not bullying you."

His words really touched a nerve, like grinding my teeth on tinfoil. I imagined myself as a fearless, thick-skinned rhino, smoke pouring from my nostrils, ready to stand my ground against Dad.

Lord, give me the right words to say.

I took a deep breath and said, "Dad, being teased over and over, year after year, sometimes feels worse than getting punched."

Silence.

Then I said, "You asked me why I didn't tell you about being bullied at school. Now I'm telling you, and you're doing *exactly* what I was afraid you'd do."

Dad pressed his lips together. Then he asked, "And what is that?"

"You're siding with Kent again, just like you've always done."

Mom stood up, clearly uncomfortable with the conversation.

"Okay, you guys," she said, "I think we need to stop this before it gets out of hand."

"Stop this?" I said, raising my voice defensively. "Why would you stop this, Mom? You know I'm right."

She raised her eyebrows. "Watch your tone, young man."

"Well, why can't you just tell Dad what you always say to me? That you don't like it when Kent pushes me around?"

She looked shocked and embarrassed. Was it possible she'd never told Dad how she felt? There was an awkward silence. Maybe I had overstepped my bounds, but I was tired of not standing up for myself.

Then Dad surprised me. Never in a million years did I expect him to say what he did.

"Louie, I never knew you felt that way about your brother—

or me." After an uneasy moment of tension, he said, "I'm really sorry."

Wow. Did that just happen? Did Dad just *apologize* to me?

"From now on, I'll try my best to stop teasing you," he said, "and I'll talk to Kent about it, too."

Dad is actually *listening* to me—and he's gonna help me with Kent! I took a deep breath, savoring the moment, and then smiled at him. "Thank you," I said.

Dad seemed really surprised by my response. He also looked a little bit sad. "Louie, has this really been bothering you for a long time?"

"Yes. For as long as I can remember. I've been praying for a normal brother—hopefully you can help me with that, too."

Dad and Mom smiled at each other. Everyone seemed more relaxed—kind of like the calm after a storm.

I cleared my throat. "Um—Could I ask you a favor?"

"Anything," Dad said.

"Could you please not tell Kent about what happened to me today? I don't want him to embarrass me in front of his friends or anybody else."

"Understood. You've got it, buddy." Dad winked at me and said, "Take care of that shoulder, okay?"

"Thanks, Dad. I will."

Just then I heard the front door open. Kent was home from baseball practice, and the timing couldn't have been more perfect.

I ran past Kent in the hallway and took two steps at a time up the stairway to my bedroom. Even though my shoulder hurt, my happiness made the pain seem like no big deal—at least for now.

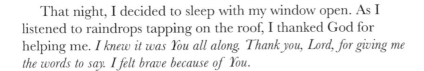

That night, I decided to sleep with my window open. As I listened to raindrops tapping on the roof, I thanked God for helping me. *I knew it was You all along. Thank you, Lord, for giving me the words to say. I felt brave because of You.*

Before I drifted off, I couldn't help but wonder what Mom would tell Mr. McCracken—and whether Eric and his friends would get suspended.

Sometimes what a person needs is not a brilliant mind
that speaks but a patient heart that listens.
— Anonymous —

15

Dirty Revenge

When I woke up the next morning, I called Nutty and told him what'd happened at school. He was *furious* and wanted to get back at Eric and his friends, but I told him to let it go—that I would deal with it in my own way. Although my shoulder was still sore and bruised after being treated like a punching bag, hearing how much my BFF cared somehow made it feel better.

Looking up recipes on the internet was a perfect distraction. Nutty and I texted back and forth all morning, sharing recipes and brainstorming about our business. Neither one of us knew what we were doing, but we promised each other to take it seriously and work as a team. Thankfully, our moms offered to pay for the ingredients—as long as we repaid them with our earnings. Whatever money was leftover, we'd split.

Nutty and I each compiled a list of our favorite dessert recipes.

Besides Gooey Chocolate Bars, my list included:

- Campfire Marshmallow Bites

- Dairy-Free Honeycomb Treats

- Red-Velvet Oozing Sponge Cake

- Dark Chocolate-Covered Pretzels

- Six-Layer Coconut Caramel Treats

- Sticky Pull-Apart Cinnamon Bread

Nutty's list, which was equally delish, included:

- Peanut-Free Chocolaty Chews
- Sweet and Tangy Lemon Bars
- Chewy Peach Cobbler Squares
- Churro Bananas with Cinnamon
- White Chocolate Cranberry Bark
- Baked Sunbutter-Stuffed Apples

When it was time to go to the cooking party, everything fell into place perfectly. We showed up at Ms. Cynthia's house at two o'clock, and the demonstration hadn't started yet. A tall, bearded chef wearing a white cooking jacket and matching hat was preparing food in the kitchen and setting up his fancy cookware.

Nutty and I had learned a long time ago what could happen if we showed up at parties without safe food to eat: an epi-pen injection for him and the squirts for me. But fortunately for us, Mom had followed through on her promise and made us nut-free, dairy-free chocolate chip cookies, which she'd wrapped in plastic. We'd hid them inside our jacket pockets just in case we couldn't eat any of the other food.

At three thirty—when the party had been hopping for at least an hour—the doorbell rang. Ms. Cynthia asked the chef, who was in the middle of his cooking demonstration, to put everything on hold for a minute.

A bunch of loud teenagers were at the door. The interruption didn't seem to bother Ms. Cynthia—but Nutty and I were annoyed because the chef had just started to make dessert. From what I could hear from the kitchen, the high schoolers had been knocking on neighbors' doors, asking for miscellaneous items from a list and then piling everything into a pickup truck. They offered to come back later, but Ms. Cynthia insisted on helping them right away.

"What else do you need?" Ms. Cynthia asked them.

I heard a bubbly girl's voice through the doorway. "We need one green sock, a silk flower, an empty milk carton, and an old toilet. Could you help us with any of those?"

Ms. Cynthia laughed like a cackling bird. "Well, I have an empty milk carton. But what on Earth do you need an old toilet for?"

A tall, thin girl with reddish hair and a ponytail on top of her head stepped into the entryway. She was outgoing and pretty but wore enough makeup to cover two faces.

"Hi, Ms. Cynthia! It's me—Olivia Fireball. We need a toilet for our scavenger hunt."

Nutty slapped my arm—the left one thankfully. "Did you hear that, Louie?" he whispered. "She's Mrs. Fireball's daughter!"

"What the—" I walked closer to the door.

"Yeah," said Nutty. "My thoughts exactly! Isn't she the one who Bobblebutt talks about all the time?"

"Yup!" I raised an eyebrow, suddenly feeling mischievous. I'd always been a rule follower, but the only thing running through my mind was a seven-letter word: revenge.

Nutty flashed me a sly grin. "I don't like that look in your eye. What are you gonna do?"

"I'm not sure," I said, rubbing my hands together, "but follow my lead. After what happened to me this week, I'm tired of being Mr. Nice Guy."

I walked across the room toward the crowd of teenagers and took a deep breath before introducing myself.

"Hey, Olivia. I'm Louie—Kent Pickle's brother."

She smiled at me and said, "Oh hey, Louie! How's it goin'?"

I could see why Kent had a crush on her, because she was really pretty—even with five pounds of makeup on her face.

"Good, thanks," I said. "Um… I overheard somebody say that you guys need a toilet?"

"Yeah!" She stepped forward. "Do you have one?"

"Actually, we have one in our backyard."

"No way!"

She was taking the bait, so I said, "Yeah! Well, my dad just replaced Kent's toilet. It's probably filthy, but it should be fine for your scavenger hunt, right?"

"Totally fine."

"Okay. Well, why don't you text Kent right now and ask if you can pick it up?"

"Right now?"

"Yeah. He's home."

"Really!" She said. "Okay. But I don't have his number."

"Let me give it to you."

I wrote Kent's phone number and our address on a napkin, shot Nutty a quick thumb's up, and then handed it to Olivia.

"You might just want to head over there and knock on the door," I said. "Here's our address. I'm sure he'd be happy to help you load his toilet onto your truck."

"That would be amazing! Thanks so much, Louie!"

"You're very welcome."

"It was really nice meeting you," she said.

"You, too, Olivia."

After the teenagers left, I turned around and high fived Nutty. "Man, I'd pay a million bucks to see the look on Kent's face when Olivia Fireball and her friends show up looking for his dirty toilet!" Both of us laughed hysterically.

Even though I knew what I'd done was kind of mean, it seemed harmless enough—and I *really* wanted to get back at Kent for all those times he embarrassed me in front of my friends, his friends, and everybody else on the planet!

———————⌇———————

When Mom and I got home after the cooking party, Dad met us at the kitchen door. He did *not* look happy. He told us how Olivia had stopped by with her friends and asked to see Kent—and his toilet. And if his narrowed eyes and fast-moving hands were any indication, I was in serious trouble.

Don't block your blessings by seeking revenge on people that wronged you.
Let it go and trust God to fight all your battles.
— *Shashicka Tyre-Hill* —

16
Moldy Soda

Sunday evening, after I'd finished doing my homework, I lay on the sofa and stared at the ceiling until everybody else went to bed. There were worse things than getting grounded, but being stripped of all electronic game privileges for a week was right up there with losing a limb. Since there was nothing else to do, I decided to check out some of the board games in Mom's tutoring studio.

Mom had painted the walls bright yellow to give it a "happy vibe" and had hired a handyman to hang up a white dry-erase board that covered one entire wall. There was a large window on the other side of the room that added lots of natural light during the daytime.

Last year, Mom went to a church rummage sale and bought three cherrywood bookshelves. She'd crammed about fifty games onto one of them, and the other two were filled from floor to ceiling with books, scratch paper, and a bunch of gadgets— including a solar-powered calculator and a cash register for kids.

Running my fingers across the game boxes, I read some titles out loud: "Cranium, Scrabble, Name That State, The Allowance Game, Pizza Monopoly, Bingo… "

Since electronic devices were off-limits and most of the games required two or more players, I grabbed a deck of cards and dealt myself a round of Solitaire. Ten minutes into the game, the snack monster in my stomach started to gurgle. So I headed to the kitchen.

I looked inside the fridge and saw a six-pack of soda on the top shelf. "Really?" I said under my breath as I reached in and touched the cold, metal cans. Mom had made it crystal clear that drinking soda would destroy your bones—and that each can has about eleven teaspoons of sugar. So why did she buy the six-pack in the first place?

I knew that drinking soda wasn't good for my body, but in my mind I'd already guzzled down an entire can.

This reminded me of what Nutty's dad had said—drink the *braaaain* juice. What if I convinced my subconscious mind that soft drinks were actually bacteria-infested, moldy beverages that were full of diseased rat poop and crushed cockroaches? Eww. I stuck out my tongue and gagged.

Well, it didn't take much to change my mind! I reached for a box of apple juice instead of soda, snuck a few bites of Dad's left-over chocolate-chip pizookie, and then went to my bedroom.

It was after 11:00 p.m., but I knew that Nutty would still be awake.

ME: Hey, dude. It worked!

NUTTY: What do you mean?

ME: I drank the *braaaain* juice.

NUTTY: You did? lol

ME: You know how much I love soda? Well, I did an experiment.

NUTTY: Really? What kind of experiment?

ME: I wanna stop drinking soda since it's loaded with sugar, so I imagined a bunch of gross stuff in it.

NUTTY: You're crazy, man. lol

ME: After I drank the *braaaain* juice, just the thought of drinking soda makes me wanna puke. Isn't that awesome?

NUTTY: You're funny!

ME: lol

NUTTY: So it really works?

ME: Totally! You've gotta try it.

I lay on my bed and thought about my brain. And then thanked God for it.

Before going to sleep, I went into the bathroom to brush my teeth. As I stared at my reflection, I couldn't stop thinking about the power of my subconscious mind. "Drinking the *braaaain* juice really does work," I mumbled, toothpaste spewing from my mouth.

If changing the way I felt about drinking soda was that easy, then maybe I could figure out a way to stand up for myself at school. What if I trained my brain to think of Kent and Eric as dumb jocks instead of intimidating bullies—would that help? And what if I asked God to protect me? I suddenly felt confident and ready to take a chance.

Imagine scooping up 7 to 10 teaspoons full of sugar
and dumping it into your 12-ounce glass of water...
that's how much added sugar is in the typical can of soda.
— Harvard T.H. Chan School of Public Health —

17

Brotherly Love

During lunch break at school on Monday, Nutty and I sat across from each other in the cafeteria. I loosened the waistband of my shorts.

"My stomach hurts," I said.

"Why, what'd you eat?" Nutty asked before taking a bite of his deli sandwich.

"Last night, I snuck a little of my dad's leftover pizookie," I said. "Now I'm regretting it."

"What's a patookie?"

"Not a patookie, dude," I laughed and shook my head. "It's a pizookie. You know, a cross between a pizza and a cookie. I think there was some milk chocolate in it."

"Oh no," he said.

"Yeah, it looks like I'll be eating the BRAT diet for the next two days."

"BRAT diet—what's that?"

"That's what my mom calls it. Whenever you have D, you should only eat bread, rice, applesauce, and toast—the acronym is BRAT."

I felt like I had a huge balloon inside my stomach, so I leaned forward and tried to get rid of the gas.

"You know…" Nutty said, a faraway look in his eyes, "we could make *patookies* and sell them. Just replace the milk chocolate with a different ingredient."

I looked at him like he was crazy. "Are you kidding? The thought of eating *pizookies* right now makes me wanna throw up."

Nutty laughed. "Dude, we'd be rolling in money. We could cover the walls and ceilings of our bedrooms with *Commander Courageous* comic books!"

Seeing Nutty so excited about our dessert business distracted me from my gut pain, so I said, "Imagine buying *anything* you want from Game Mart!"

I pretended to have a British accent and mimed tossing video games into a shopping cart. "Yes, here's one for you, one for me, one for you, one for me. Oh, let's take all of it—every last video game in this store! Here's my credit card."

We laughed so hard the other kids in the cafeteria gave us weird looks.

Suddenly, Nutty's face froze. He looked past me and said, "Don't turn around. It's Bobblebutt, and he's coming this way."

What? It didn't make any sense. Kent's high school was all the way across town.

"Why would he be here?"

"I don't know." Nutty whispered, "But your brother looks really mad."

I heard Kent call out to me. "Louie!"

I turned around in my seat to face him. "What are you doing here?"

Kent stood with both hands on his hips and scowled. "We have to leave."

My stomach acid was working overtime. "Leave? But school's not over."

"Just get your things and come with me. *Now.*"

Nutty and I exchanged bug-eyed looks, which set us both off into a frenzy of nervous giggling.

"That does not look like brotherly love." Nutty said between snorts.

Kent had already walked halfway across the cafeteria. He turned around and yelled, "Now!"

Not all storms come to disrupt your life.
Some come to clear your path.
— Blossom Chukwujekwu —

18
Payback Time

I grabbed my backpack and followed Kent to the faculty lot, where his car was parked in the loading zone.

"Hurry up!" Kent said.

Why was he so demanding? As soon as I strapped on my seatbelt, Kent turned up the music and peeled out.

Nervously I asked, "Where are we go——"

"Stop talking."

During the entire ten-minute drive, he didn't say another word. Why was he so mad at me? Did it have something to do with the toilet prank? I didn't ask. I just held tightly onto my backpack, leaned against the car door, and said a quick prayer.

I kept thinking about a quote that Mr. Green had written on the whiteboard in science lab. It was from some guy named Zig Ziglar, and it was about how the acronym F-E-A-R could mean two different things: "Fear Everything and Run" or "Face Everything and Rise." And then it said, "The choice is yours." Now, more than ever, I needed to make a choice: continue running from Kent's bullying——or grow thicker skin, like a rhino, and ask for God's help. So I drank the *braaaain* juice and convinced myself to "Face Everything and Rise."

Kent pulled off the road onto an uneven, gravelly driveway near Old Man Joe's Tire Shop. Gnats and mosquitoes buzzed around us, and swirling dirt clouds billowed around the car, so I rolled up my window. We passed a broken-down barn near the trailhead, where pepper trees swayed in the wind. Everything looked so peaceful—but warning bells were going off in my head. Why was my brother taking me out here?

Kent pulled over and parked the car. Then he turned to look at me for the first time.

"Why did you do it?" he yelled.

We were sitting so close to each other, I could see the whites of his eyes getting bigger.

"Do what?" My voice cracked.

He slammed his fist on the steering wheel. "Don't play dumb! Why did you give Olivia Fireball my phone number and tell her to pick up my crappy toilet from the house?"

"Oh, that. Sorry," I said, cowering against the passenger-side door. It suddenly felt claustrophobic in the tiny sedan.

"Louie, do you realize what you've done to me? Do you have any idea how social media can destroy a person's reputation in high school?"

I got a sinking feeling in my stomach. And it wasn't a pizookie-related gut issue. No, my stomach was churning with a mixture of fear and guilt at what I'd done to my brother.

Kent sighed. "You've put me in a very bad position, Louie. So you and I need to deal with this, once and for all."

He got out of the car and motioned for me to follow him. It looked like he was on the verge of crying.

Wow. What I did must've really upset him. And, for the first time in my life, I actually felt bad for Kent.

I got out of the car and followed him into a clearing. A small run-down outbuilding could be seen in the distance. A dozen black-and-white cows were grazing in the grassy field, but nobody was around—nobody but Kent and me.

Great. He's gonna feed me to the cows because I shamed him with a dirty toilet.

But Kent kept walking toward the tiny wooden building, which looked at least a hundred years old. As we got closer, flies swarmed around our heads and a putrid odor caused my gag reflex to spring into action. And then it dawned on me. It was an outhouse! *Gross.*

Where was a barf bag when I needed one?

Kent motioned for me to walk closer to him. We pushed our way through tall bunches of grass to get to the door. He pulled back a metal latch and the door flew open with a loud *crack!* I jumped backwards and fell to the ground.

Kent pointed inside the outhouse, which was covered from floor to ceiling with scaly snake skins. It must've been a molting room, and I had a bad feeling some snakes were still slithering in dark corners.

"Get in there," he said.

I knew I had to do it. Otherwise, Kent might wrap me in the snakes that belonged to those skins! But how could I? Inside that outhouse was a rotted-wood toilet with a rusty metal seat—and a black hole below that led to who-knows-where.

"Now sit on that toilet and say you're sorry," he demanded.

"I'm not gonna sit on that disgusting thing!"

"If you *don't* sit on that toilet right now and apologize for humiliating me in front of my friends, then we'll just have to move onto Plan B."

Plan B? Oh, crud. What could possibly be worse than Plan A?

"If you don't," he continued, "I'll make sure that your stupid desserts won't have the best customer reviews, if you catch my drift."

"You wouldn't!"

"Yes, I would. Try me."

"And how would you do that?"

He smiled. "Social media."

Touché. Bad reviews on social media would destroy our business.

"Okay, okay," I said, "You win."

Pinching my nose, I pushed past the creaky door—trying not to step on any snakes—and sat down on the vomitrocious toilet.

Then I said, "I'm really sorry that I embarrassed you with the toilet prank, and I promise never to do it again. There—I did it. Now can we go?"

75

Kent crossed his arms. "That's not good enough."

"What do you mean? Come on!" I pleaded. "I did what you asked."

Kent's foot was propping open the door to the outhouse. He pointed at me and said, "From now on, I will get *twenty percent* of your earnings from the cookie business."

"No way!" I yelled.

The rancid odor from that outhouse may have been burning my nostril hairs, but that was *nothing* compared to the flames I felt burning a hole in my wallet. My anxiety was rising to panic level, so I whispered a quick prayer. "God, please give me the courage to stand up for myself."

What happened next changed everything.

God never sends you into a situation alone.
God goes before you. He stands beside you.
He walks behind you. God is with you.
— Anonymous —

19

Forgive Him

The rusted toilet creaked beneath me as I shifted on the filthy metal seat. I still couldn't believe that I'd agreed to squeeze my body inside of that revolting outhouse. I wasn't sure if I was more freaked out about the foul odor coming from the toilet or the snakes that could strike at any time from the black hole below.

"C'mon, Louie." Kent said, blocking the doorway. "Give me twenty percent, and we'll be even."

Even. Really? After all the times he'd bullied me over the years?

I imagined Nutty's and my dessert business failing before it even started—the feeling was a billion times worse than getting punched by Eric Peevy. As I pinched my nose with one hand and swatted flies with the other, I visualized throwing a can of moldy soda, loaded with a special blend of dead cockroaches and rat poop, at Kent's face.

But then I thought about it. I mean, I *really* thought about it.

We'd been enemies for far too long, and it was time to shift the energy. So if giving Kent that money would change the way he treated me—if he stopped bullying me—then it would be worth every penny.

And if I didn't agree to Kent's terms, maybe our relationship would never improve. We might never get along; we might always hate each other—*forever*. Was I willing to let that happen? Nope. Having a brother—a real brother—suddenly meant more to me than anything. I guess praying about it helped me to recognize that.

I thought about the *braaaain* juice experiment with the soda.

Part of my twisted brain actually believed that mashed bugs and bacteria were swirling around inside each can—bizarre. So maybe it was time to try another experiment. I knew that I could change a habit—like drinking soda—by convincing myself to see things differently. So was it possible to switch my negative feelings about Kent? Tell myself that we were friends—and convince myself that it's true? It was definitely worth a try.

So for the first time ever, I pictured myself laughing with Kent, playing video games with him, hanging out with our friends at the movies, and eating dinner without fighting. Then I took it one step further—*I forgave him* for all that he'd done to me. It was the strangest yet most freeing feeling! I even thought about hugging him, but that would've been too weird.

Being friends with Kent was definitely a tall glass of *braaaain* juice to swallow. But if Nutty's dad was right about my subconscious mind—if part of my brain could believe anything I told it to be true—then I was willing to convince myself that I had a *normal* relationship with a *normal* brother. And I hoped that Kent would eventually believe it too.

What if he wasn't an ogre after all? What if Big-Burly-Bruiser-Bro was just a mixed-up kid who was jealous of my friendship with Nutty? Did he actually enjoy bullying me, or was it just a way to hide his feelings?

I'd known that sending Olivia Fireball and her friends to our house was going to embarrass Kent, but I didn't see the big picture—how he'd be shamed on social media. The more I thought about it, the worse I felt. There was so much more at stake than losing a little bit of money. I could lose my brother.

Mom had said that Kent and I should resolve our problems by talking to each other, but I'd been too scared of him to try. I still was. I needed help, so I decided to pray.

God, is there any way
that you can possibly add
forgiveness to my mad
brother's brain today?

How should I pray?
Because I'm really sad
that I've never had
the right words to say.

Will there ever be a day
when Kent and I will have had
a relationship that's not bad?
Will everything be okay?

Is there a price I should pay?
I do agree with Nutty's dad,
that my attitude can make me glad.
Will braaaain juice keep the anger away?

Since Nutty and I are only in seventh grade, our dessert business—let's be real here—won't be a life-long thing. We're not gonna make *that much* money. So if giving Kent twenty percent of my future earnings will help us to become friends, then I'll do it happily and thank God every single day.

Suddenly, surviving middle school seemed much less important than having a bully-free homelife with a nice brother. Now *that* would be life-changing.

I looked at Kent to test the *braaaain* juice, and sure enough, I saw him differently now—we were friends. And it was time to play a game with him.

"Okay, how about ten percent?" I asked.

"Twenty percent or no deal."

"Twelve percent?"

"Twenty."

My acting skills were only so-so, but this back-and-forth thing was pretty funny considering I probably would've given Kent *any* amount of money he wanted. Having a real relationship with my brother was priceless. Now I just needed the guts to tell him to stop bullying me. My underarms started sweating.

"Fifteen percent," I said.

"Twenty."

"Seventeen."

"Twenty percent or we move onto Plan B."

"Fine! Twenty percent! But only if you promise to stop picking on me! I'm sick and tired of being bullied by you, especially since I haven't done anything to deserve it."

Oh my gosh, I said it! *Thank you, God.*

Kent looked at me for a minute with an unreadable expression on his face. Then I saw a little smile turning up the edge of his mouth.

"Well, okay," he said. "Let's shake on it. And nobody can know about this but us. That includes Dad, Mom, and Nutty. Deal?"

Kent had agreed to stop bullying me. Hold on—

KENT AGREED TO STOP BULLYING ME?

Wow. Time to celebrate! All that I needed to do was ask!

I thought about Zig Ziglar's quote and decided to "Face Everything and Rise."

"Deal."

We shook hands, and I think both of us were surprised—and relieved.

As Kent drove me back to school, I saw the sun peeking through the clouds and smiled; I knew that everything was going to be okay. Kent and I had come to an agreement, and having thicker skin gave me more strength than I'd ever imagined. *Thank you, God, for giving me the courage to do what was right.* And I was definitely relieved that Kent didn't drop me into the black snake hole or feed me to the cows.

What is broken can be mended. What hurts can be healed.
And no matter how hard it gets, the sun will rise again.
— *Meredith Grey* —

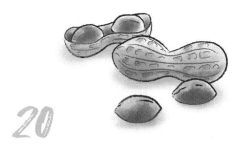

20

The Big Bad Wolf

Kent dropped me off at school just before the end of lunch period. As I got out of the car, he said, "Remember to keep this between us, all right?"

"Yup. Got it," I gave him a thumb's up.

I ran to history class and slid into my seat behind Nutty, who spun around and looked at me with bulging eyes. "Are you okay?"

"Yeah." I smiled vaguely and pulled out my history book. "Everything's fine."

Nutty lowered his eyebrows. "Really? Where did he take you?"

"On a drive."

"A drive?"

"Yeah." I tried my best to avoid eye contact.

"Where?"

"Around the corner."

Nutty was getting frustrated. "Dude, the suspense is killing me! What happened?"

"I don't really wanna talk about it, okay?"

He leaned back in his chair and looked at me with narrowed eyes. "Why aren't you telling me what happened, Louie?"

I sighed. "Sorry, but I can't."

"Why not?"

"Because I promised Kent I wouldn't say *anything* to *anybody*."

"So you're not gonna tell your *best friend* why Bobblebutt dragged you away from school today?" His face was getting redder by the minute.

Nutty and I had never kept secrets from each other, but honoring my promise to Kent was part of growing thicker skin. I needed to hold up my end of the deal—even if it meant upsetting my BFF.

I shook my head and said, "Sorry, dude. Please don't take it personally. He was just angry about the toilet, but now we're good."

The whites of Nutty's eyes were turning bloodshot red—if he were *Commander Courageous* steam would be pouring out of his ears! "You *seriously* expect me to believe that?"

I felt trapped, but what else could I do? Thankfully the bell rang, so Nutty was forced to turn around—but not before angrily pushing my history book onto the floor.

If I told Nutty that I'd secretly agreed to pay Kent twenty percent of my earnings, then our dessert business would be over before it started. And if Kent found out I'd told Nutty, he'd smear our desserts on social media and nobody would buy them; we'd have no money for comic books or video games, and Nutty would be mad at me anyway. So even though Nutty would probably never understand, I decided that protecting the reputation of our business was the best choice. Hopefully he won't hold a grudge against me for too long, but with his intense personality, he'll probably give me the silent treatment for a while.

When I first started calling him Nutty instead of Nathan, he thought it was funny coming from me because I also had problems with food. But when other people teased him about his peanut allergy—*watch out!*

Last year in sixth grade, a bunch of us were eating lunch in the cafeteria when the Big Bad Wolf, Eric Peevy, walked by with his annoying friends. They had always teased us about our food allergies, and one of them threw peanut shells at Nutty's food tray.

"Hey, Peeee-nutty! Want some peanuts with your lunch?" Eric and his wolfpack laughed and high fived each other as they strutted past our table.

Nutty was fuming. His face was the same color as the red delicious apple in his hand. Without missing a beat, he stood up and rocketed the partially eaten apple at Eric's head. Unfortunately, Nutty had never been much of a baseball player, and Mrs. Fireball just happened to be walking toward us with a fresh cup of coffee. She was talking on her cellphone when the apple smashed into her Styrofoam cup, splashing hot coffee all over her.

"Aaauuggh!" she shrieked. "My coffee! My dress!"

Nutty tried to explain, but Mrs. Fireball was too angry to listen. "And when you're done mopping up this mess," she yelled, pointing at him with a shaking finger, "Principal McCracken will expect you in his office!" She stormed off, still wiping the brown liquid from the front of her pink dress.

Nutty told me afterward that Mr. McCracken hadn't been too hard on him, because of his own daughter's peanut allergy. He'd just asked him to report it the next time someone bullied him instead of throwing things. But to this day, Nutty's still peeved at Mrs. Fireball for making him clean up the mess.

We found out later that Eric Peevy and his cronies were suspended for two days. They were also required to watch a five-minute video on YouTube about the seriousness of food allergies and the dangers of cross contamination. *Awesome!*

Since then, he hasn't thrown anything at anyone. That's what you call progress.

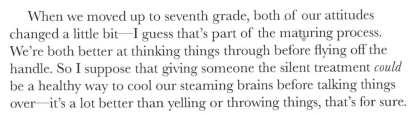

When we moved up to seventh grade, both of our attitudes changed a little bit—I guess that's part of the maturing process. We're both better at thinking things through before flying off the handle. So I suppose that giving someone the silent treatment *could* be a healthy way to cool our steaming brains before talking things over—it's a lot better than yelling or throwing things, that's for sure.

I was fully prepared to accept Nutty's silent treatment and

handle it like a thick-skinned rhino. I tried putting myself in his shoes and could definitely understand why he was so upset— but I wanted him to get over it soon so we could see the opening of *Lizard Man Returns* this weekend.

Over the next few days, I texted Nutty several times to apologize, hoping that he would let it go. But he didn't respond.

Repeat this to yourself: Today, I will not stress
over things I cannot control.
— Anonymous —

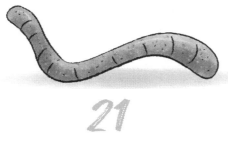

21

Red Licorice and Gummy Worms

The rest of the week was grueling—I had to see Nutty every day at school but he never acknowledged me. Then on Saturday morning, Nutty finally broke down and texted me back, and we agreed to disagree about my promise to Kent. Even though he was defensive at first, I could tell he was excited to get together again.

We met at his house and then rode our bikes to the movie theater. At around eleven o'clock, the place was already jam-packed with people waiting to buy tickets. It was opening weekend for *Lizard Man Returns*, so little kids dressed in lizard costumes were running all over the place. I couldn't wait to go inside—their screams were annoying.

When Nutty and I walked into the lobby area, the smell of freshly made popcorn turned my stomach.

"Gross," I said, pinching my nose. "That popcorn smells awful!"

Nutty looked shocked. "How could you not like popcorn? You've always liked popcorn!"

"Yeah, but lately butter's been bothering my stomach," I said. "Plus, I'd rather eat a box of red licorice anytime."

Nutty stuck out his tongue and scrunched up his face. "Red licorice? Eww!"

"My mom eats an *entire* box of red licorice during the trailers—even before the movie starts!"

"Are you serious?" Nutty coughed and clutched his throat, pretending to gag.

"Yep. And I love 'em, too." I laughed. "So if *she* can do it, then *I* can do it."

"But red licorice is totally gross," Nutty said, "and red dye number forty is gonna kill you guys."

"Well, how about the *fake butter* on your popcorn?" I asked, pointing to the concession stand. "That stuff will send you to the grave."

We both laughed.

"I guess we might as well die happy!" I said.

I'd missed joking around with Nutty. Laughing together felt good.

The theater manager stood up on a chair and yelled into the crowd with a megaphone, "Grab as much popcorn as you'd like, because it's Free Popcorn Day! Thank you for choosing our theater to see *Lizard Man Returns*, and be sure to tell your friends!"

A mob of people pushed to the front of the line to grab the prefilled bags. Greasy popcorn overflowed onto countertops and spilled onto the floor while teenage employees ran around with brooms and dustpans, trying to keep the place clean.

Nutty and I eventually made our way to the front of the line where he reached for a bag of free popcorn and I bought a box of red licorice for five bucks. And for the next two hours, Lizard Man destroyed San Francisco on the movie screen while Nutty shoveled popcorn into his mouth and I gobbled up an entire box of red licorice.

After the movie, we headed to the lobby. "Wasn't that awesome when Lizard Man *devoured* everybody in the trolley car?" Nutty said.

"Yeah, man!" I dropped my empty licorice box in a trash can.

"Dude, look." Nutty tapped my arm and pointed across the room. "It's Ames." She was walking toward us.

"Hey, you guys!" As usual, Ames was wearing a baseball cap. "What'd you guys see?"

Nutty stretched out his arms and roared. *"Lizard Man Returns!"*

"Me too! We were in the front row 'cause my grandma can't see that well."

Then Ames turned and faced me. "Hey, Louie."

I tried to act casual but my cheeks felt hot. "Oh, hey."

"I still have your cooler," she said. "I picked it up that day in the cafeteria and then forgot to give it to you."

Awkward. I didn't want Nutty to tease me about my blushing. "Oh, it's not a big deal," I said. "I have another one. Thanks, though."

That afternoon, while doing homework on the sofa, I began to think about how much fun Nutty and I'd had at the movies... and drifted off to sleep thinking about popcorn and candy. I dreamed I was back at the theater buying a gigantic bag of gummy worms from the concession stand. I knew they were loaded with processed sugar and food coloring; but after popping that first watermelon-flavored worm into my mouth, I couldn't stop. I kept reaching for more, grabbing handfuls of blueberry, mango, strawberry, and pineapple chewy delights. And then, in the blink of an eye, they were gone—the bag was empty.

At first, my dream body seemed fine with all that sugar. I felt great! Yet as the gummies squeezed their way through my digestive system, it started to feel like a high-speed train was racing through my veins. The sugar was causing my heart to beat ten times faster than normal, and I felt my life-force draining away...

I startled awake, sweaty, heart still pounding. The experience had felt so real. I'd wiped out an entire gummy worm colony in one sitting! It reminded me of the disturbing dream about the beekeeper, and I felt disoriented and depressed for the rest of the afternoon.

Later that night—while Dad and Kent were watching a baseball game on TV and Mom was folding laundry on the sofa—my gut started to hurt. I loosened my pants but still felt uncomfortable. A huge gas bubble was growing inside of my stomach, causing it to pooch outward, and the only way to release it was—well, *you know*. So I stayed in my room and played with Hershey and Dusty.

Although my body might look healthy on the outside, filling my gut with a whole box of red licorice sticks sure didn't do my insides any favors. What if I made a sweet, healthy snack to bring to the movie theater next time? That way both Nutty and I could chow down without polluting our bodies with too much food coloring and other crud. Plus, we'd save money in the long run. Inspired, I hopped on my computer and searched for more recipes.

Willpower is a muscle; the more you use it, the stronger it gets.
— *Matt Molnar* —

22
Pay Attention

On Sunday morning, we went to church and sat near the front of the sanctuary. Bright beams of light followed the band members on stage as they sang upbeat Christian music. Everything about it stimulated my senses.

But when the pastor started talking, I got antsy—crossing my arms, looking down at my feet. Although I could hear his words, I kept getting distracted by a voice inside my head. Dad noticed I wasn't paying attention.

"Louie, are you listening?" Dad whispered.

Busted. I looked up and gave him a thumb's up. He raised his eyebrows and pointed at the stage, a hint that I'd better stay focused—or else. The "or else" usually meant the loss of video game privileges, so I sat up and tried to listen.

But the voice inside my head kept butting in. It was like a broken CD player that was stuck and spinning—playing the same song over and over again.

When will this be over? Can we leave yet?

When will this be over? Can we leave yet?

Since I was sitting between Dad and Mom and didn't want to get in trouble, I pretended to pay attention, but controlling this seventh-grade brain was nearly impossible. Then it occurred to me that I might be able to do two things at once—listen to the pastor's sermon and daydream about other things! I decided to test this theory and imagined watching a series of movies while still trying to take in the pastor's words.

Imaginary Movie #1:

Nutty and I ride our bikes to Twice-As-Nice-Movies, a jumbo-sized movie theater where everything's doubled in size. Single-serving containers of popcorn are twice as big as the ones at our theater. Salty pretzels, fresh out of the oven, look like mini loaves of bread. Red licorice sticks are twice as thick, and there are 48 of them in each package. Soft drinks are served in one-liter bottles so nobody asks for refills (since their bladders are twice as full). Nutty and I lounge in huge, cushiony recliner chairs and wait for the double feature to begin. I turn my head to my left—and Ames is seated next to me, holding my hand! Since both movies are shown at the exact same time, in the exact same room, but with two different screens, the three of us constantly turn our heads back and forth, left to right, watching both films simultaneously...

Imaginary Movie #2:

Nutty and I escape from church and ride our black stallions to the nearest bakery, where the owner says we can borrow his kitchen for an hour, as long as we clean up afterwards. Our goal is to make five hundred chocolate chip cookies, so we need to move fast. White baking flour is flying everywhere, raw eggs are slip-sliding off countertops, and the first batch of cookies is burned— but we laugh hysterically! After cleaning the kitchen and packing hundreds of cookies in plastic wrap, Nutty and I hop onto our horses and gallop through town with wind rushing against our faces. We pull back on the reins and stop in front of Fresh Market, where hundreds of people are throwing money at us, begging to buy our chocolate chip cookies. I notice Ames is in the crowd, and she blows me a kiss. I lift her up onto the back of my horse, and the three of us ride off to Game Mart for an unbelievable shopping spree...

I didn't realize I'd drifted off until Mom leaned in and whispered, "Thank you for trying to pay attention, Louie. After church, we'll have lunch with your grandparents. And then we can go home and make one of your desserts, okay?"

Did she just say that we could make one of my desserts? Awesome! I wanted to stand up and yell, "Yes! And the crowd goes wild!" But instead I whispered, "Sure. Cool." Mom smiled and gently kissed my forehead. I desperately wanted to sneak out of church, but since that was out of the question, I continued my imaginary adventure series.

Imaginary Movie #3:

I am wearing lightweight, futuristic body armor with a heat-resistant apron wrapped around my torso. In the blink of an eye, I'm teleported to another universe to fight against fiery dragons, using steak knives, metal spatulas, and silicone oven mitts. After defeating the towering lizards and rescuing Queen Ames and her royal court, I level up in the game, unlock the stone oven, and cook fiery dragon stew...

"Bum-bum-buuuuummmm!" I whispered.

Dad grabbed my hand firmly and gave me the *look*.

I sat on my hands. "Sorry!"

Pointing to the pastor, Dad mouthed the words, "Pay attention."

But how could I concentrate when Mom said we'd be baking dessert after church? The voice inside my head started up again.

When will this be over? Can we leave yet?

When will this be over? Can we leave yet?

The band had just finished playing its last song, so thankfully the church service was almost over. My brain was tired from transporting me to different places in my imaginary movies. And I'd learned that it's not possible to listen to a sermon and daydream at the same time.

Maybe Nutty would like to come over after church to help make the dessert. So I texted him to find out.

It all begins and ends in your mind. What you give power to has power over you, if you allow it.
—Leon Brown—

23

Blue Eyes and Butterflies

Mom and I were in the kitchen making the dough for Sticky Pull-Apart Cinnamon Bread when the doorbell rang.

"I wonder if that's Nutty," I said. I hadn't seen a reply to my text about him coming over, but maybe I'd just missed it.

Mom looked at her watch. "Well, it's definitely not one of my students, because today's Sunday."

She wiped both hands on her apron and disappeared around the corner. The click-clack of her high-heeled shoes became more faint as she walked down the hallway, then stopped when she reached the front door.

"Who is it?" I heard her ask.

I leaned against the kitchen doorframe and craned my neck to listen. It was probably one of Kent's dumb friends. As I turned my head toward the entryway, a slightly familiar, high-pitched voice became more clear.

"Hi, Mrs. Pickle. I'm Amy Marie—uh, Ames. Is Louie here?"

What? Why was Ames here? Suddenly my head felt like a pressure cooker, and the kitchen was a hundred degrees hotter.

"Well hello, Ames!" I heard Mom say. "It's so nice to meet you." She invited Ames to come inside the house. "Let me get Louie."

I ran into the bathroom and looked at myself in the mirror. No stinkin' way—you've got to be kidding me. Besides my hair being a total mess and being covered in dough, I was wearing Mom's Minnie Mouse apron with red bow ties and frilly edges. I tore the apron off my body, threw it on the floor, and then washed my hands.

"Louie, where are you?" Mom's voice was getting closer.

I looked below the sink and saw a plastic bottle next to Mom's brush. Hair gel. Maybe that would make this mop look presentable. I pumped a handful of pink gel into my hand and smeared it across the top of my head, but not only did it make my hair look worse, now I smelled like old lady perfume! A glob of pink gel dripped off my forehead.

Mom knocked on the door. "Louie, are you in there?"

"Um—yeah, Mom. Just a sec."

Panicked, I reached for some toilet paper to clean up the gel and knocked over the plastic bottle. And in an attempt to catch it, I tripped over the floor mat, banged my knee against the wall, and then hit my head on the towel rack. Yet somehow I managed to catch the bottle of pink hair gel just as it was landing inside the toilet bowl—and my entire hand and arm followed. Toilet water splashed onto my face and shirt, and I fell backward onto the floor, groaning.

"Louie, are you all right?" Mom pushed open the door.

And standing next to Mom? Ames. With my lunch cooler in her hand and a shocked expression on her face. She turned red and averted her eyes.

Great. I'd made a complete fool of myself in front of Ames. Falling into a toilet and being seen drenched in that water was *ten-quintillion times worse* than sitting on an outhouse toilet surrounded by snake skins. My head started to spin... and then everything went dark.

"Louie, are you okay?" Mom sounded faraway. And worried.

She mumbled something about fainting and then asked Ames to grab a wet washcloth. I felt woozy and lightheaded, but the cool water helped me to relax. I opened my eyes. I was lying on the bathroom floor, staring up at the ceiling. I turned my head and saw the most beautiful blue eyes looking at me.

"Hey, Louie. Are you okay?"

It was Ames. She wiped my forehead with a wet washcloth and smiled.

Was I dreaming? Time stood still—but my heart was beating so fast.

I think I'm in like.
How could it be?
Why are there butterflies
fluttering inside of me?

She's like a breath of fresh air,
with blue eyes that care,
even with pink, gooey gel
and toilet water in my hair.

I think I'm in like.
But how could it be?
Yes, she's definitely for me.
This must be why people write poetry.

After cleaning up the bathroom mess, I ran upstairs to my room, changed into a clean shirt, and then scrubbed the nasty toilet water off of my face. I threw my wet shirt and Minnie Mouse apron into the laundry basket and then ran downstairs to the kitchen, where I could hear Mom and Ames talking.

When I walked into the room, Ames was seated on a barstool at the counter.

"Hey, Louie! Your mom invited me to stay for dinner." She stood up and smiled, looking relieved that I was okay.

I walked over to the refrigerator, trying to act casual. "Hey." Flames of heat torched my cheeks—I couldn't get myself to look at her.

Mom broke the tension by throwing a hand towel at my face. "Catch!" she said, with a giggle in her voice.

I reached up, grabbed it, and then threw the towel to Ames,

who snatched it with both hands. She laughed and then ran a circle around the kitchen, as if running bases at a baseball game.

Mom caught up with her, snagged the towel, and then tossed it back to me. All three of us were in hysterics, which was a perfect way to get past the bathroom fiasco.

Mom disappeared for a moment into the dining room and came back holding two aprons.

"Here you go! Now you guys can bake cookies together while I prepare dinner." Mom saved the day—yes! Although, I was a little bit disappointed we didn't get to finish the cinnamon bread.

"Also, I have a surprise for you, Louie."

Mom reached into the hall closet and pulled out a medium-sized box with international shipping labels on top. I looked at her and smiled—wondering what was inside.

Sometimes the bad things that happen in our lives put us directly on the path to the best things that will ever happen to us.
— Nicole Reed, Ruining You —

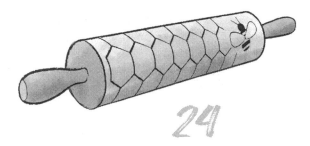

24

Mr. Smarty Pants

The cardboard box was dented on all four sides, which wasn't unusual since it had come all the way from Poland. I worried that Mom's surprise might be damaged, but when I opened the package, a bubble-wrapped rolling pin was inside—and it was in perfect condition.

"Surprise!" Mom said. "You can use it for your desserts."

At first I wasn't quite sure what to say... and then it hit me. "Ohhh, I get it. Thank you, Mom—that's awesome!"

Mom was grinning from ear to ear. "It's my pleasure, Louie."

After the bee invasion and my beekeeper nightmare, I guess Mom took me seriously when I said I wanted to make a difference and take care of the bees.

Bee and honeycomb patterns were laser-engraved all over the rolling pin. They were meant for imprinting dough with bee and honeycomb shapes. Ames and I took turns oohing and aahing over it.

Ames said, "Remember how you told us we should bake allergy-friendly desserts for the science fair? This gadget could help us make fancy cookies, giving us a better chance of winning the contest!"

I agreed with her a hundred percent.

A sugar cookie recipe was included with the rolling pin, but the baking instructions had been translated from Polish to English. Ames and I were in hysterics over the gazillion grammar mistakes and spelling errors.

Also, the measurements were listed in grams—not cups. But instead of freaking out about it, I took Mom's advice and looked up "grams to cups conversion" on Google.com.

Instead of making a batch of cookies right away, we decided to read the instructions first and figure out how to convert the ingredients. If we had time, we'd bake some goodies. If not, we'd pretend to mix everything in a make-believe batter bowl.

I took my time reading the ingredient list aloud, since I didn't want to embarrass myself in front of Ames by stuttering.

BUTTER

"Well, we'll be using a butter substitute, but the amounts will be the same. So 200 grams of butter equals about 0.9 cups or $\frac{9}{10}$, which is less than 1 cup."

"Wow! You're really good at math," she said.

"Thanks." I blushed and kept my eyes on the paper.

Mom chimed in. "And if you add melted butter to the mixture instead of using solid butter, then the cookies will be too soft and gooey."

I didn't know that. "Then we'll definitely need to use unmelted butter for the recipe."

"Absolutely," said Mom. "Also, I read that salted butter isn't always fresh, because the salt acts as a preservative."

Ames frowned and said, "What's a preservative?"

"It's something that's been added to prevent decay," said Mom. "The fresher the ingredients, the healthier the cookies. You can include that information in your science fair presentation."

SALT

"We also need to add a pinch of salt," I said. "It's easy enough with the salt grinder."

Mom handed the salt dispenser to Ames, who pretended to grind a couple twists of salt into the invisible mixing bowl.

OIL

"We'll need 2 tablespoons of olive oil." I looked at Mom. "But won't olive oil make the cookies taste nasty?"

She smiled with a twinkle in her eyes. "You're absolutely right, Louie. Olive oil does have a strong flavor, which may overpower the sweetness of your cookies. Maybe we should use corn oil instead?"

"Let's try it!" I opened the pantry door, grabbed corn oil from the second shelf, and handed it to Ames. "Here you go."

"Thanks!" Ames seemed to be enjoying this. "Do you have any measuring spoons?"

The cylindrical utensil holder was on the countertop. I spun it around until the stackable measuring spoons stopped in front of Ames.

"Here," I said, "use these."

She grabbed the spoons and pretended to pour 2 tablespoons of oil into the batter bowl.

EGG

Mom looked over my shoulder and read the directions.

"The recipe calls for one egg," she said. "Be sure to crack it open into a little glass bowl, so none of the shell will get into the mixture."

"I've never done that before," said Ames.

Mom nodded. "If there's a bad odor or if it looks discolored, then you'll have to throw away the egg."

"Makes sense," Ames said.

"And if the egg is spoiled," Mom warned, "then what do you think would happen to the mixture?"

"Trashola," I said, trying to be funny.

"Yep. You're absolutely right, Louie. The contaminated egg would ruin the food and make everybody sick."

"Down the drain it goes," I joked.

FLOUR

I continued reading the recipe. "We'll also need 400 grams of fine wheat flour."

I pulled up the conversion chart on my phone, typed 400 grams into the cups section, and hit enter. The metric conversion was 3.2 cups. "We don't use decimals with measuring cups, but I can convert it to a fraction."

Ames didn't say anything. I think my math skills impressed her.

I felt my face get warm but tried to stay focused on the recipe. "So if 400 grams equals 3.2 cups, then the equivalent fraction would be $3\frac{2}{10}$ cups. We don't have measuring cups in tenths, so if we reduce the fraction we get $3\frac{1}{5}$ cups."

The room was quiet. I looked up and noticed that Ames's mouth had dropped open and Mom was beaming with pride.

I felt a rush of happiness. "And since $3\frac{1}{5}$ cup is less than $3\frac{1}{4}$ cup by a smidge, then we can just measure $3\frac{1}{4}$ cup and take a little bit out."

Mom was the first to speak. "Great job, Louie. I know how much you enjoy math, so this is a perfect recipe for you."

Ames clapped and congratulated me. "You'll need to show me how to use that conversion chart, Louie."

"Sure!" All of this positive attention was helping me forget my earlier embarrassment.

Ames walked toward the pantry and asked, "By the way, do you have gluten-free flour?"

"Yeah, we do. My mom uses gluten-free flour to make stuff for my dad because he can't eat anything with wheat."

"No way—neither can I!" Her eyes widened. "Gluten gives me migraine headaches."

"Really! My dad gets those, too!"

"That's cool," said Ames. "It looks like your dad and I are in the same club!"

I looked at Mom. "Then we'll need to make some gluten-free cookies so Ames can eat them too. Can we make both?"

"Sure!" Mom pulled down a bag of gluten-free flour from the top shelf. "I have both kinds of flour in the cupboard. Just be careful of cross contamination because we don't want anybody to get sick."

Ames grinned. "Awesome! Thank you, Mrs. Pickle." Then she high fived me. "Thanks, Louie." It was cool how comfortable she seemed with us.

SUGAR

"There's one more ingredient on the list," I said. "We'll need 150 grams of icing sugar."

Ames scrunched up her forehead. "What's icing sugar?"

"Do you wanna look for us?" I asked, handing her my phone.

"Sure." Ten seconds later, Ames yelled, "It's powdered sugar!" She turned red, clearly embarrassed by the volume of her voice.

"Don't worry about it, Ames," Mom said, working her magic. "I love your enthusiasm!"

Using the conversion chart on my phone, I selected "grams to cups" with powdered sugar and typed 150 grams as the portion; up popped 1.2 cups.

"Okay, you guys," I said. "It looks like 150 grams of powdered sugar equals 1.2 cups or $1^2/_{10}$ cups or $1\frac{1}{5}$ cups. That means it's a smidge less than $1\frac{1}{4}$ cups."

When I finished reading the recipe, it hit me—my dyslexia hadn't slowed me down! Woohoo!

"Well, thank you, Mr. Smarty Pants!" Mom said, tossing me a hand towel.

Then the three of us ran around the kitchen throwing it back and forth. We were out of breath from laughing when the doorbell rang.

The great thing about new friends is that they
bring new energy to your soul.
— *Shanna Rodriguez* —

25

Betrayed?

Ames was standing beside me when I opened the front door. Nutty walked into the entryway and gave me a fist bump. Then he turned toward Ames with a surprised look on his face and said, "Hey, study partner!"

For a moment, I forgot to breathe.

"Study partner?" I asked, narrowing my eyes.

Nutty flashed his dimpled smile at Ames and said, "Yeah, we had fun!"

"You did?" I suddenly wanted to kick him out of my house.

"Yeah," said Nutty, "we talked about the science fair project."

My ears were getting hotter by the second. "When did you do that?"

"During lunch break," he said.

"Lunch break?"

"Yeah. Remember when you and Bobblebutt left campus at lunchtime?"

"Who's Bobblebutt?" Ames asked.

"It's Louie's older brother, Kent—aka... Bobblebutt."

Ames laughed loudly and clapped her hands. "That's funny!"

It definitely seemed like Nutty was trying to show off in front of her.

"Yeah, dude," Nutty continued, "after you left, I saw Ames sitting by herself in the cafeteria. So I asked if she wanted to talk about our science fair project."

He looked at Ames, who smiled back at him.

I just stood there glaring, jaws clenched.

Were they *flirting* with each other? Nutty knew that Ames and I had become friends, and it didn't take a rocket scientist to figure out that I was starting to like her. So here's the million-dollar question: Why did my so-called best friend decide to hang out with her behind my back and then tell me about it *afterwards?* If he'd asked me about it first, I would have told him I liked her and that she was off-limits—not that she was mine or anything, but he would've understood.

Now, I wanted nothing to do with him; it almost felt like he'd betrayed me. Losing our friendship over a junior high crush was crazy to imagine, and would totally go against the BFF code, but I felt like my hopes had just been flattened by a concrete paver.

Nutty looked over at me, and his eyebrows shot up.

"Um, dude? Do you have a sec?" He motioned toward the hallway.

Ames rolled her eyes. She jogged back to the kitchen and said, "I'm gonna help your mom. See ya in there."

"What's up with you, man?" Nutty asked in a whisper.

"What do you mean?" I asked defensively. "What's up with you?"

"Dude, you're looking at me like I stole your *Commander Courageous* comic book. Why are you so mad?"

I stared directly into his eyes and said, "Do *you* like her?"

"Who—Ames?" Nutty held up his hands. "No, dude! She's not even my type."

Silence.

Nutty studied me with an expression on his face that I'd never seen before. Then he gave me a sly grin. "Do *you* like her?"

All of a sudden, I felt really stupid. If I had just taken the time to ask Nutty and not assume the worst, then none of this would've happened.

"Um—yeah. I think so." There. I said it. How embarrassing.

I couldn't believe I actually told him—or anyone—about Ames. "Sorry for getting mad at you."

"Why are you sorry, man?" Nutty laughed and put his arm over my shoulder. Then he dropped his voice to a whisper. "We've never talked about *girls* before—now I know your type." Then we exchanged fist bumps, and Nutty jogged back to the kitchen.

I stood in the hallway, waiting for my racing heart and blushing cheeks to calm down. Somehow I needed to find two seconds of courage—just enough to walk back into that room with my head held high.

Life's too short to argue and fight. Count your blessings, value your friends, and move on with your head held high and a smile for everyone.
— Mhar —

26
Food Fight!

When I walked back into the kitchen, the countertop was covered with baking supplies—sugar, flour, measuring cups, a stainless steel mixing bowl, spatulas, my new rolling pin, and a mat for rolling the cookies.

"Where have you been, Louie?" Mom asked.

"Uh, nowhere," I said, exchanging glances with Nutty.

"Really?" said Mom skeptically. "Well, we're glad you're back, because now we need you to help with the dessert."

Mom cranked up some rockin' music on Spotify. I could tell she knew that something had happened in the hallway and wanted to change the vibe in the room.

"All right, you guys," said Mom, as she danced across the kitchen floor, "let's get this party started!" She used a wooden spatula as a pretend microphone and sang off key to the music.

At first, Nutty and I were totally embarrassed. But when Ames started dancing with Mom, we had to join in, too. We were bumping into each other and laughing until our stomachs hurt.

Before long, Ames was dancing next to me. She jokingly bumped shoulders with me, laughed, and circled around the room with her hands in the air. She must've put a magic spell on me, because even though it was my bad shoulder, I felt no pain. It was one of those perfect moments that you wish would never end. Ames was dancing in my kitchen, and Nutty finally knew how I felt about her.

"Your mom's pretty cool, Louie," she said.

"Thanks."

When the song ended, Mom untied her apron, picked up her car keys, and walked toward the garage.

"I just remembered that we're out of butter, so I'll need to swing by Fresh Market. Be back shortly, Louie. Okay?"

"Sure, Mom."

"Will you be able to manage everything while I'm gone?"

I gave her a thumb's up.

As soon as Mom's car disappeared around the corner, Nutty's demeanor changed. He jumped onto the countertop, legs dangling, and yelled, "Food fight!" Then he reached into a bag of flour and plopped a fistful onto my head!

"Dude," I said nervously, brushing the flour out of my hair. "What are you doing? My mom's gonna be back soon!"

"Lighten up, man. It'll be *fun!*" he said with a wink and a nod toward Ames.

Having a food fight with Ames and Nutty in my own kitchen did sound pretty exciting! Sure, I'd probably get grounded—but in that moment, I didn't care. I said a quick prayer and hoped that Mom would forgive us for destroying the kitchen and wasting food. Then I opened up the pantry door, pulled a box of fruity cereal from the shelf, and started throwing handfuls at both of them!

Ames yelled, "Did someone say *food fight?* Awesome!" She looked around for something to throw.

Nutty jumped off the countertop. He reached into a basket near the kitchen sink, grabbed a ripe tomato, and then smashed it on top of Ames's head! Red tomato juice poured down her hair and face—it was hilarious!

Ames rushed to the refrigerator, scooped up a tray of eggs, and started launching them at us—*Crack!* Slimy egg white and sticky yolk dripped from my hair and apron. "Gotcha!" she laughed while reaching for another one.

Ames was making me nervous. "Please don't break *all* of them! My mom will freak out if we don't have enough for the cookies!"

But Ames and Nutty were having too much fun to listen to me.

So I decided I didn't care either. The three of us were having a blast—and there was no turning back now.

When Ames pulled back her arm to fire the last egg, Nutty lunged toward her and blocked it with his arm. The egg dropped to the ground and broke—*Splat!*

With all the commotion, we didn't hear Mom's car pull into the driveway. But when she opened the garage door into the kitchen, everybody froze. Nutty, Ames, and I were covered from head to toe with oozing egg, squishy tomato chunks, rainbow cereal, and white flour—and so was the kitchen.

"What on Earth—" Those were the only words that came out of Mom's mouth, but the look of disappointment on her face said so much more.

We were so busted! Thankfully Mom was forgiving. We apologized, cleaned up the mess, and faced the consequences—which included not making cookies that night. Mom also said we'd need to pay her back for the wasted food as soon as we earned money from the dessert business.

"You have a dessert business?" asked Ames, trying to act serious despite the wet tomato juice dripping from her chin.

Nutty and I looked at each other and laughed. I knew exactly what he was thinking and was on the same page. It was obvious that Ames was now one of us and that we should invite her to be part of our friend group.

"Ames," I said, "since you'll be working with us on the science fair project anyway… would you also like to help us with our dessert business?"

Her eyes practically popped out of her head. I could see the whites all the way around them.

"Are you serious? Totally!" She high fived both of us with her sticky hands.

The total cost for one tomato, a dozen organic eggs, a bag of gluten-free flour, and a box of cereal was twenty bucks. We promised to pay it back as soon as possible…

Later, as I was getting ready for bed, Mom came into my room and talked to me about the food fight. She said, considering all that I'd been dealing with this past week, the mess would stay between us—that Dad and Kent didn't need to know about it. Mom to the rescue—*again*. Once I was under the covers, I thanked God for answered prayers and an awesome mom—and then fell asleep with the biggest smile on my face.

You've gotta dance like there's nobody watching, love like you'll never be hurt, sing like there's nobody listening, and live like it's heaven on earth.
— William W. Purkey —

27

I Love You More

The next morning, I woke up in the best mood—until I sat on my bike and noticed it had a flat tire. Great. Happy Monday. I tried to inflate it with our bike pump, but the handle was broken; Kent probably ran over it with his car.

So I woke up Mom and asked her to drive me to school, which worked out fine because I was able to thank her again for keeping our secret.

"So you're really not going to tell Dad or Kent about the food fight?"

"Of course not," she reassured me. "My lips are sealed." She twisted an invisible key on her mouth and pretended to throw it out the car window.

I was relieved. "Thanks, Mom."

"Louie, I know that you've been dealing with some tough stuff lately. How's that shoulder?"

"It's much better, thanks."

She pulled up to an intersection near school and waited for the light to turn green. "That's probably because you hung out with Ames yesterday."

"*Mom!*" What was she, a mind reader?

"It's okay, Louie." She laughed. "I like Ames. She's a nice girl."

Blushing, I muttered under my breath and looked outside the passenger window.

Then Mom said, "So—would you guys like to try again?"

"Try what?"

"Baking cookies for your science fair project."

I turned back toward Mom. "Really?" After yesterday, I was surprised she'd let the three of us anywhere near her kitchen.

"Well, you *did* apologize, silly," she said. "And you guys *did* clean up the mess. Plus, you promised to reimburse me for the food. So I don't see why not. Unless, of course, you don't *want* to get together again with Nutty and Ames."

I couldn't contain my excitement and beamed. "No, no! That would be fine."

Mom's demeanor suddenly shifted. Her smile disappeared—she looked serious. Was she changing her mind? She took a deep breath, looked straight into my eyes, and said, "But *only* if you promise to smash another dozen eggs in the kitchen." Silence. Then she stuck out her tongue and said, "Gotcha!"

Both of us laughed—I mean, *really* laughed! So hard that tears filled our eyes.

"And this time," Mom teased, "would you please actually *make* some cookies?"

We laughed the rest of the way to school. Mom was still trying to catch her breath when I hopped out of the car in the parking lot.

"Thanks for the ride, Mom."

"You're welcome, Louie."

I grabbed my backpack and grinned at her. "I love you."

She looked at me with the kindest eyes. "I love you more."

For a split second, I didn't want her to leave—we were having so much fun together. And for the very first time, I realized that Mom was my friend, too.

Just before she drove off, Mom called out, "By the way, if you and your friends need to work on your science fair project, you can use my tutoring studio tonight!"

I couldn't believe my ears. "Okay! Thanks, Mom. I'll tell 'em."

I jogged to the quad area and looked for Nutty, but he'd already gone to language arts class. So I went there, too, and texted him.

ME: Hey, dude.

NUTTY: Hey, man. What's up?

ME: Food fight! lol

NUTTY: Haha! Did you get the eggs out of your hair?

ME: Yeah, after washing it thirty times! You?

NUTTY: Nope. Still have egg shells in my ears.

ME: lol

NUTTY: Do you have flour up your nose?

ME: No!

NUTTY: I do. Is your mom still mad at you?

ME: Nah. She was fine.

NUTTY: Really? My mom would've grounded me for life!

ME: lol

NUTTY: Sooo you like Ames…

ME: I guess. Yeah.

NUTTY: That's awesome!

ME: Do you wanna work on our science fair project tonight?

NUTTY: Tonight? Sure. How about Ames?

ME: Do you think we should add her to a group text?

NUTTY: Good idea.

ME: I mean, so we can include her.

NUTTY: Yeah, okay.

ME: Do you wanna get her number? Or should I?

NUTTY: lol

ME: What?

NUTTY: *You* like her, dude, not me!

ME: But what should I say?

NUTTY: Tell her what you told me.

ME: That I like her?????

NUTTY: No! Tell her about the science fair project.

ME: Oh, okay. My mom said we can use her tutoring studio to work on it.

NUTTY: Awesome.

ME: And she said we can bake cookies again as long as we don't have another food fight! lol

NUTTY: Your mom's so cool.

ME: Yeah, thanks.

NUTTY: Okay. Gotta go. See ya at lunch.

As a mother comforts her child, so will I comfort you.
— Isaiah 66:13 (NIV) —

28
Sweaty Palms

It was time to drink the *braaaain* juice again. I needed to pour some positivity into my stressed-out head. Ames would be okay with me asking for her phone number, right? I mean, why wouldn't she? After all, she *did* come over yesterday to drop off my lunch cooler, and she *did* stay for the food fight. Either way, I needed to find out, and I was hoping that Nutty would help me.

When the lunch bell rang, I grabbed my backpack and hustled to the lockers—I was starving. Since I didn't see Nutty right away, I devoured my deli sandwich while I waited for him outside, in front of the cafeteria.

During those minutes alone, my anxiety ramped up. How could I possibly text Ames? I knew it had to be done since our science fair project would be due soon and all three of us needed to work on it together, but texting a girl—especially a girl I *liked*—was totally out of my comfort zone.

That's when I noticed Ames. She was stretched out on the grassy area underneath a huge oak tree, using her backpack as a pillow. It looked like she was wearing earbuds and rockin' out to some music, because her baseball cap kept moving back and forth to a beat. She seemed perfectly content by herself, which was cool. I admired her from a distance, wanting to say hello but unable to put one foot in front of the other. Instead, I hummed an alphabet poem about her:

As she rocks to the beat
Below that shady oak tree
Courageously I take a peek,
Determined not to look so meek.
Embarrassed 'cause Ames is sweet...
(What rhymes with sweet? Meat, sheet... feet!)
Funny, smart, and quirky with Skechers on her feet.

Get moving, Louie; stop acting like a dumb sheep.
Have some guts; face your fears; don't be a wimpy geek.

Is there a chance that she'll bake cookies and study with me?
Just thinking about asking her makes my stomach feel weak.

Kitchen ingredients we'll combine to make dozens of treats,
Large batches of yummies baked on metal cookie sheets,
Mixed together like ooey, gooey, rich, and chewy sweets.
Never-ending laughter, while whippin' up desserts to eat.

Oh, what will I do if Nutty doesn't show up today?
Please give me the strength to ask Ames anyway.
Quickly I'll text her; maybe she'll say, "Sure, okay."
Relief and extreme happiness is how I'd feel all day.

Should I walk over there and stand by the oak tree?
Tempted to speak... but what if I act like a dorky sheep?
Underneath this geek, thick skin like a rhino runs deep.

Very happy that Ames thinks I'm smart as can be,
Wondering if she senses my fear and anxiety.

X-static that my new friend, Little Bo Peep (with)
Yellowish hair and braces on her teeth (will)
Zip through life as my good friend for keeps.

Suddenly, almost as if she could hear my thoughts, Ames sat up and turned my way. She smiled, waved in my direction, and then grabbed her backpack and ran toward me.

"Hey, Louie! How's it going?"

"Great, thanks. How about you?" *Please, God, let there be no salami or lettuce stuck in my teeth.*

"Good, good. Are you feeling better after that fall yesterday?" she asked.

My face turned three shades of red. "Oh, yeah. I'm fine, thanks." How embarrassing—she brought up the bathroom disaster.

Ames leaned forward and whispered, "Don't worry about it," her blue eyes twinkling in the sunlight.

"Thanks," I mumbled, desperate to change the subject. "So, Nutty and I are gonna work on the science fair project tonight."

"Cool!"

My palms started sweating.

Then she said, "I wanna help, too!"

"Uh—really? Oh, okay. Great. My mom said we can use her tutoring studio for our science homework."

"That's rockin' awesome! I really like your mom."

"Thanks. She also said we can bake cookies."

"Another food fight! *Yes!*" Ames pumped her fist and then laughed. "Just kidding."

Then she said, "Do you have your phone, Louie? That way we can text each other. It would probably be easier."

Her words were like music to my ears. "Um—yeah." I unlocked my phone and handed it to her.

Ames added her name and phone number to my contacts list. "Let me know when I should be there tonight, all right?"

"Sure. I'll send a group text to you and Nutty."

She grinned and hugged her backpack to her chest. "Perfect! Thanks, Louie. I'll talk to you later." Then she slung her backpack over her shoulder and ran to class.

Wait till Nutty hears about this—that I drank the *braaaain* juice and followed through with getting Ames's phone number! Well, Ames was actually the one to bring it up, but who cares! This was shaping up to be the best day ever!

Face your fears. Courage is like a muscle that needs to develop slowly.
— *Jim Burns* —

29

Baking Cookies

After dinner, Nutty and Ames came over to work on our science fair project. We had decided to dive into the baking portion of our project first, since we knew that it would bring us one step closer to teaching that jerk-wad Eric Peevy—and any other bullies who might be listening—about the seriousness of Nutty's peanut allergy. Time to strap on Mom's frilly aprons and get cookin'!

The three of us were going to work in different areas of the kitchen, because we were making different recipes and wanted to avoid cross contamination. Mom and I had set up each workstation with these supplies:

stainless steel mixing bowl (1)

long wooden spatula (1)

glass measuring cup (1)

metal cookie sheet (2)

wired cooling rack (2)

plastic spatula (1)

wet ingredients

dry ingredients

For all the recipes, we used rice milk instead of cow's milk and margarine instead of butter, since Mom hardly ever buys dairy products. We had to share the silicone oven mitts and the oven timer, which buzzed every fifteen minutes. One by one, we took turns staring through the oven window—waiting for our desserts to turn golden brown. And when they were done baking, we set the cookie sheets on wired cooling racks.

The house started to smell like a bakery. And every so often Dad, Mom, or Kent would wander into the kitchen and ask if they could sneak a taste.

"Nope," I said with a big smile. "We'll need *all* of these for our science fair project. If there are any leftovers, then you can try one."

Dad and Mom were pretty understanding, but Kent—not so much. He threw his hands in the air and muttered, "Thanks for nothing," before grabbing a bag of potato chips from the cabinet and storming out of the kitchen.

Nutty, Ames, and I looked at each other, rolled our eyes, and cracked up. We laughed until we cried, just like when we had our food fight.

Then Nutty said, "These chocolate cookies smell so good. I wanna eat one *right now!*"

"Don't you dare!" Ames yelled. "We should wait until all the recipes are done, and then taste them together."

We were having such a great time that, for a split second, I was tempted to start another food fight. But Mom would be furious. And she'd probably never allow me to have friends over again. So rather than ruining it for everybody, I focused on my recipe.

I added raw honey in place of sugar to sweeten my honey-comb dessert recipe because I wanted to show people that honey is both tasty and healthy for our bodies. Then, using a spatula, I combined all the ingredients together in my mixing bowl. Now all I needed to complete my recipe were a silicone rolling mat and my new wooden rolling pin. As soon as I leaned on the rolling pin and flattened the dough ball, images of bees and honeycombs were imprinted into the doughy cookie mixture. "Check it out!" I called to the others. "This is awesome!"

Nutty and Ames circled around my work station. We oohed and aahed over the cute little buzzers.

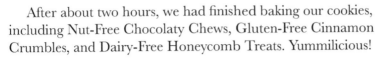

After about two hours, we had finished baking our cookies, including Nut-Free Chocolaty Chews, Gluten-Free Cinnamon Crumbles, and Dairy-Free Honeycomb Treats. Yummilicious!

"How are we gonna make sure we have enough pieces?" Nutty asked. "Mr. Green said that there'll be seventy-five people at the science fair, and I bet everybody will want to try our cookies."

"I think Louie should figure it out," Ames said. "He has the math brain." She pointed to my head and winked.

I was thrilled that Ames considered me the smart one. And even though Nutty hates math, I hoped his feelings weren't hurt.

"Well," I said, "First we need to figure out how many cookies we have in total. I made two dozen. How about you guys?"

"I made two dozen as well," said Nutty.

"Me, too," added Ames.

"So each of us made twenty-four cookies. If we cut each one into four bite-sized pieces, then we'll have more samples to share." I wrote some math equations on a piece of paper.

24 cookies x 4 pieces = 96 bites (Nutty)
24 cookies x 4 pieces = 96 bites (Ames)
24 cookies x 4 pieces = 96 bites (Louie)

$$
\begin{array}{r}
96 \text{ bites} \\
96 \text{ bites} \\
+ \ 96 \text{ bites} \\
\hline
288 \text{ bites}
\end{array}
$$

"That equals 288 pieces," I said. "So if we divide 288 pieces by 75 people, then we can figure out how many bites each person could eat." I wrote another equation on the piece of paper.

$288 / 75 = 3.84$

"That's about three pieces per person," I said. "So if all seventy-five people eat three pieces, then there will be plenty of leftovers for us!" We high fived each other and laughed.

Using kitchen knives, we divided each cookie into four pieces. Then we separated the Chocolaty Chews, Cinnamon Crumbles, and Honeycomb Treats into three different bowls and covered them with plastic wrap.

While Nutty was cleaning the mixing bowl in the sink, he tried to smear raw cookie dough in my hair. But Ames didn't want me to get in trouble again, so she talked him out of starting another food fight.

Alone we can do so little; together we can do so much.
— *Helen Keller* —

30
Snorting Like A Pig

Even though we'd cleaned up, the kitchen still smelled really good.

Nutty was drooling over the cookie samples. "Let's try some already!" he moaned.

"Wait!" said Ames. "Before we do, we should label everything." She scribbled words onto sticky notes and attached them to the bowls. "This one's peanut-free, this one's gluten-free, and this one's dairy-free."

Then she picked up a small piece of her Cinnamon Crumble and took a bite. "Oh my gosh! This cookie is *totally sick!*"

Sick? I didn't know what that meant, but Ames looked happy, so I figured it was a good thing.

Nutty took a bite of his nut-free cookie. "Mmm, these choco-laty chews are *sick*, too!" He tried holding back a laugh, but crumbs flew out of his mouth, causing Ames to laugh so hard she started snorting like a pig—which made the three of us laugh even harder. Still giggling, we put some cookie pieces on a plate and jogged down the hallway toward Mom's tutoring studio.

Mom was just finishing up her last tutoring session. "Hey, guys!" she said. "Come on in. We were just leaving."

Then Mom looked at me and said, "Louie, I bought the supplies you needed for the science fair project. Everything's in the closet. Let me know if you need anything else." She disappeared around the corner with her student.

Hershey and Dusty, who had followed us into the studio, made themselves comfortable under the table.

Ames smiled. "Aw, your dogs are really cute." She looked around the room. "I've never seen a whiteboard that big! Can we draw on it?"

"Sure," I said, "use those dry-erase markers."

Ames drew pictures of wheat, milk, and peanuts on the board. "We should draw these on the poster board," she said.

"Sounds good to me," said Nutty. "Why don't we split the poster board into three sections—dairy for Louie, gluten for Ames, and peanuts for me."

"Didn't Mr. Green tell us that the contest would be judged on creativity?" I said.

"Yeah," said Nutty.

My brain was spinning. "Then why don't we get more creative?"

"How?" asked Ames.

"Well, I've been thinking about it," I said. "What if we used somebody's camera phone to make a short movie about our gut issues? Nutty could talk about his peanut allergy. Ames, you could talk about your gluten sensitivity, and I could talk about my lactose intolerance. And while our movie's playing, people could eat cookies and look at the poster board."

Nutty grinned. "That would be awesome! And we should throw things at each other during the movie—kind of like a food fight. So when Louie's talking about diarrhea, Ames and I could chuck toilet paper at him!" He pretended to throw a roll of toilet paper, like a quarterback with a football.

"Yeah!" said Ames. "And Louie and I could throw peanuts at you!"

I cracked up, and Ames snorted like a pig again.

"I'm serious about the toilet paper!" Nutty said, trying to keep a straight face. "But no peanuts."

Ames yelled out, "I know! I know!" and then high fived him. "Let's do it!"

After we sat down at the table, Nutty said, "I'm gonna talk

about my peanut allergy and how much it annoys me when people treat me differently."

"Dude," I said, "you can't do that. We wanna win this contest, don't we? We want our cookie business to be featured on the cover of the magazine."

Ames frowned. "Wait—why not? Why can't we tell people that we're annoyed? I think we should be real and tell them how we feel. We could still win."

She had a good point. "All right. Then what's the purpose of our science fair project?"

"To let others know that we're not different. I mean, why should it matter that we have food allergies or gut problems? Everybody has issues. Just because we can't eat certain foods, does that mean we should be pushed around for the rest of our lives?"

Nobody said a word. For the very first time, we understood that there was more at stake than just winning a contest—ending the bullying was the ultimate prize. And if we wanted to make more friends at school, something would have to change; otherwise, eighth grade would be ten times more twisted than seventh grade.

"Okay, so if we do this," I said, "the video can't be too long."

Nutty nodded. "Yeah, we should keep the video short."

Ames got up and paced in front of the window. "Our poster board should have sciencey diagrams, charts, and descriptions of gut issues. And the video should be funny—something about foods we *can't* eat, places we *can't* go, and how we have *no* control over it. Also, I think we should wear matching t-shirts with red slash marks through the foods we can't eat."

Nutty slapped his hands on the table and leaned forward. "I *really* don't want you guys to throw peanuts at me in the video. The *last* thing I need is for Eric Peevy and his stupid friends to think it's okay for them to do it too."

"We won't—promise," said Ames. "What if we hand you a jar of peanut butter instead?"

Nutty smiled. "That'll work."

"Dude, say something funny about your peanut allergy on the

video," I said, trying to reassure him. "Then people will laugh *with* you—not at you."

"Yeah," he said, "you're probably right. I'll try. Maybe there are other people at school, who have similar issues. Maybe we can start a food allergy club, where people can talk and cook and eat together—instead of feeling like we're all alone."

Ames nodded enthusiastically. "I think a club like that would be really nice." She paused. "Because I don't have that many friends."

Ames sat down and the three of us began drawing pictures of food and taping artwork to the poster board. After a few minutes of working quietly, Ames said, "If you guys are wondering why I don't have any friends, I don't mind telling you."

"Yeah. Okay," I said. Nutty and I had always been curious about why she ate lunch alone—but were too uncomfortable to ask her about it.

"My best friends and I used to get pizza every Friday night," she said. "But then I started getting bad headaches. I found out that gluten was the cause, so I couldn't eat pizza anymore. And since I didn't want them to miss out on pizza night, I just told them to go ahead without me. To be honest, I was really hoping that they'd say, 'No, we wanna be with you. Let's find another place to hang out. We can find a different restaurant.' But that never happened, and it hurts. Sometimes I hear them at school talking about how much fun they have together, and I just don't feel like I fit in with them anymore—so I kind of make myself look busy a lot. That's why it's really cool that I met you guys, because you accept me for who I am."

The three of us looked at each other, and none of us said a word. We understood each other's pain. The silence was a little uncomfortable, but not like the awkward feeling you get when you like a girl. It was more like Nutty and I cared about her as a person—like the sister we never had.

That was the moment Nutty, Ames, and I became best friends. None of us said it, but we all felt it. It was really cool—strange, but cool, mostly because she was a girl. And even though she was my first middle school crush, I realized that her friendship was more important—that way the three of us could feel like best friends *together.*

"Let's do this, you guys!" Nutty said.

Ames and I gave each other fist bumps. "Yeah! Let's do this!"

Friends are angels who lift us to our feet when our wings
have trouble remembering how to fly.
— *Anonymous* —

31

Food Hurts

The next day, I spoke with Mr. Green after class. He seemed pretty cool about the change to our science fair project.

"As long as food allergies and digestive problems are still your *main* focus—not just bullying—then it's fine."

"Great!" I said, "Also, we'd like to bring some homemade dessert samples for everybody to taste. We made peanut-free, gluten-free, and dairy-free cookies."

"Excellent! I can't wait to try some. It looks like your team's gonna hit this one out of the ballpark!"

I couldn't wait to tell Nutty and Ames what Mr. Green just said—it sounded like we might have a chance of winning the science fair contest! And since the whole town received a free subscription to *River Valley Magazine*, if we were one of the winners, everyone would read about us and we'd get free advertising for our desserts. And because everybody knew somebody with food allergies, our sales would skyrocket.

After school, we got together at Nutty's house to shoot the videos. Ames surprised us with matching t-shirts, which her mom had made using iron-on patches.

"Check these out!" she said.

Nutty grumbled. "Do I really have to wear a smiling *peanut* on my shirt?"

"Dude, it looks good on you," I said. "At least you don't have to wear a fat *cow* on yours!" I pointed to my shirt and mooed.

"Well," said Ames, "I'd rather be a peanut or a cow, instead of a dorky strand of *wheat!*" She rolled her eyes and we all laughed.

We changed into our goofy t-shirts and took gobs of selfies. The pictures were hilarious, so we decided to edit them into the beginning of our video once we were done.

I told them what Mr. Green had said, and we high fived each other.

"Hey," I said, "Do you guys mind if we name our business Bee Safe Cookies? That way people will know we're selling healthy desserts with honey in some of them."

They both agreed.

"And we should give a title to this project," Nutty said. "How about *Peanuts, Gluten, and Dairy: When Food Hurts?*"

"That's Awesome!" Ames said. "And what about the club name? How about the Bee Safe Club?"

Nutty and I yelled out, "Yes!" And then all of us chanted loudly, "*Bee Safe! Bee Safe! Bee Safe!*"

When it was time to shoot the video, everybody agreed to be real. We were nervous at first, but it didn't take long to get comfortable because we kept cracking each other up!

And since we'd planned on throwing things at each other during the video, all of us brought props.

SCENE 1:

CAMERA SETUP:

The three of us stood together wearing our matching t-shirts. Nutty put his camera on a tripod and hit the record button. Everybody took turns speaking.

ME:

Our science fair project is called Peanuts, Gluten, and Dairy: When Food Hurts. In this video, Nutty, Ames, and I will tell you about our personal experiences.

NUTTY:

You'll learn about food allergies and intolerances - or
things that our bodies can't digest - and how they're not
fun and are sometimes even scary.

AMES:

Although everybody may not be able to eat the same
things, we hope you'll think twice before joking about
serious food issues.

ME:

Also, we've started a new dessert business called Bee
Safe Cookies for anybody with food allergies. Please try
the samples. I made Dairy-Free Honeycomb Treats.

NUTTY:

I made Peanut-Free Chocolaty Chews.

AMES:

And I made Gluten-Free Cinnamon Crumbles.

ALL OF US:

Together, we can "Bee Safe" and healthy.

SCENE 2:

CAMERA SETUP:

The next scene was mostly me. Nutty and Ames hid off
camera throwing rolls of white toilet paper back and
forth. As the rolls unraveled they draped long strips of
toilet paper across my shoulders and head, which made
me laugh so hard I could barely get through my speech.

ME:

Hi, I'm Louie. Everybody gets stomach aches. But if
your gut swells up like a balloon after you've eaten
a slice of cheese pizza, or if you get stomach cramps,
diarrhea, nausea, or gas after eating certain foods,
then you might want to reconsider your diet. If your
body is sensitive to dairy, then I understand how you
feel because lactose intolerance is a pain in my gut.
I have a hard time digesting ice cream, grilled-cheese

sandwiches, tacos with sour cream, spaghetti with parmesan cheese, strawberry cheesecake, pizza, or anything buttery that comes from a cow. Why? Because my gut is the boss of me, and staying away from dairy is the only way to make it happy. Yeah, it's not easy. And when people tease me, it feels ten times worse.

Whenever I eat or drink anything with dairy, my small intestine freaks out and doesn't know how to break down the milk sugar, or lactose, because it's missing an enzyme. If I could control my small intestine, it would be a miracle. But since I can't control my organs, please don't tease me about having an angry intestine.

Oh, and since we're talking about bullying, please stop treating me differently because of my dyslexia. I know that my reading problem is off-topic, but— whatever.

Enjoy these dairy-free cookies, which I made for you.

NUTTY:

(walks into scene and offers me a glass of milk)

ME:

(putting up my hand) No thanks.

NUTTY:

(turns and walks away)

SCENE 3:

CAMERA SETUP:

The next scene featured Ames. Nutty and I hid off camera throwing slices of bread back and forth. Sometimes we'd purposefully hit her in the head, but she tried to stay focused. Then Nutty grabbed an entire loaf of bread and threw all the pieces at her at once, which made Ames start snorting like a pig again.

AMES:

Hi, my name's Amy Marie—Ames. Have you ever had a really bad headache? One where sounds make your head pound, light makes it feel ten-thousand times worse, and you feel sick to your stomach? Those are called migraines. I used to get them all the time until I found out about my gut problem. Whenever I eat foods with gluten—like mac 'n' cheese, cookies, cakes, bread, or pasta—my stomach gets bloated. Then I get a headache, which turns into a horrible migraine. The pain in my head makes me feel nauseous, so I crawl into the bathroom and vomit. And on top of everything else, I get diarrhea, which is pretty awful. Nothing—not even watching TV, playing video games, or sleeping—gets rid of that awful migraine, so I hide under the covers in bed and feel miserable. Sometimes, when the pain is out of control, I end up in the emergency room.

Why does this happen to my body? Well, gluten is a protein found in foods like wheat, rye, and barley. If I eat anything with gluten, then my small intestine goes whacko. Part of my gut gets damaged, so food doesn't digest properly, which causes diarrhea—not fun.

After watching this video, hopefully you'll understand that even though I can't eat certain foods—like pizza for example—we can still hang out and have fun. I'm really grateful to my new friends, Louie and Nutty, who accept me for who I am.

Enjoy the gluten-free cookies that I made for you.

ME:

(walks into scene and offers her a loaf of bread)

AMES:

(putting up her hand) No thanks.

ME:

(turns and walks away)

SCENE 4:

CAMERA SETUP:

The next scene featured Nutty. Ames and I stayed in the background, waving protest signs that we'd designed

the night before. We'd drawn red circles with red diag-
onal bars through pictures of peanuts and peanut
butter and jelly sandwiches and had written the words
Severe Allergy: No Peanuts Please underneath.

NUTTY:

Hey. My name's Nathan. I'm allergic to peanuts—
I mean, deathly allergic to peanuts. So you'll never see
me eating peanut butter and jelly sandwiches, peanut-
flavored ice cream, or trail mix with peanuts. I also
don't drink smoothies or shakes with peanuts. That
means I need to avoid bakeries, ice cream stores,
smoothie shops, and restaurants that fry food with
peanut oil. I also have to read every label on boxed
foods. So if the ingredients aren't listed, then I won't
risk it.

How can eating even a peanut crumb hurt my body?
Well, if the tiniest piece gets mixed into my salad,
or any other food, many things would happen fast.
It's called anaphylaxis. I'd start coughing, itching,
and vomiting. My throat and tongue would swell up,
breathing would become difficult, and my organs would
slowly shut down. That's why I carry emergency medicine
with me all the time—because it could save my life.

So for those of you who like to throw peanut shells at
me in the cafeteria, now you know why it's not funny—or
safe. Please stop bullying me and others who have
health issues.

Enjoy these peanut-free cookies that I made for you.

AMES:

(walks into scene and offers him a jar of peanut
butter)

NUTTY:

(putting up his hand) Heck, no!

AMES:

(turns and walks away)

134

SCENE 5:

CAMERA SETUP:

In the final scene, Nutty, Ames and I were standing together.

AMES:

Thank you for watching our video.

NUTTY:

By the way, all of these cookies were made in the same kitchen. Louie, Ames, and I were careful not to cross contaminate the food. So, yes, it's possible to become friends with people like us—we won't bite you.

ME:

Remember to try our Bee Safe Cookies! And if you have food allergies or gut sensitivities, check out our Bee Safe Club.

ALL OF US:

Thank you!

Laughing makes everything easier, funnier, and happier,
especially when you do it with your best friends.
— Anonymous —

My 'Twisted' Life in Middle School

32
Science Fair Disaster

On Friday morning, all of the students were excited—and nervous—about the science fair. Since it was one of the biggest days of the year, team members were allowed to arrive early to set up their projects in the gym. There was definitely a competitive energy in the air.

Nutty, Ames, and I were wearing our matching t-shirts. Some kids gave us weird looks—and a couple of them even mooed when they saw my cow t-shirt—but it didn't bother us. Mr. Green liked our creative idea, and that was all that mattered.

Mr. McCracken looked very principalish, circling the auditorium with a clipboard in hand, telling everybody where to set up their projects. We were assigned to a table directly across from Eric Peevy and his immature friends—yay—who put together a bizarre project called "Elephant Toothpaste." They must've been feeling good about their chances because they were body slamming into each other and laughing from the moment they arrived. I got a sinking feeling in my stomach.

Mr. McCracken saw them messing around and said in a loud voice, "Eric, Jack, Ryan—settle down."

Eric apologized with zero sincerity. "Sorry, Mr. McCracken."

Jack and Ryan mimicked him. "Yeah, we're sorry, Mr. McCracken."

I could tell none of them were really sorry, but Mr. McCracken just shook his head and walked away. I guess he didn't have time to police them while judging the contest, but as soon as he left they continued to be obnoxious.

The journalist from *River Valley Magazine*, a short, round woman, walked around the gym looking at all the science fair projects. I studied her from a distance; she asked lots of questions and made eye contact with every kid. Hopefully, she wouldn't like any of their projects better than ours.

Nutty poked me. "Dude, what are you doing? We need to set up our display."

"Oh, sorry," I said, still distracted. I really wanted to win that contest.

Ames handed me a bowl of cookies. "Earth to Louie. Take these and put them somewhere, please."

After we'd set up our poster board, positioned the tablet for the video, and put out the three bowls of cookies, we stood next to our table and waited for the journalist to circle around to our area.

Nutty smiled confidently. "We've got this."

I didn't want to say anything to burst his bubble, but it wasn't looking good for us. Sure, we'd worked hard on our science fair project—but lots of other people had too.

Two teams were set up next to Eric's table: one was using a mini-roller coaster track with noisy wheels to show friction, and the other was conducting some kind of electricity experiment with smoke coming from a black wired box. One row over people were oohing and aahing when they saw a moldy bread experiment and a messy volcano erupting.

I watched Eric and his dumbo friends struggle to set up their elephant toothpaste display and wondered why they were wearing eye goggles, rubber gloves, and trash bags over their shirts. When I overheard them complaining about not having enough space, I imagined a huge elephant stomping through the gym while they attempted to brush its teeth—so I burst out laughing.

Eric glared at me and said, "You gotta problem, Pickle?"

"Uh—no."

"Good," he said with a sneer, "then turn your ugly cow face around and stop looking at us. Or else I'll turn it around for you." He punched the table with his fist.

"Ignore him," Nutty said quietly.

Easy for him to say. He wasn't the one worried about getting punched again. I started thinking about Mom's conversation with Mr. McCracken—how Eric probably blamed *me* for getting him suspended even though he was the one who hit me. I'd told Mom I didn't want her to say anything to Mr. McCracken, but I understood why she did. If only there could've been a way to tell the principal about Eric without turning it around on me.

I did some deep breathing exercises, because my heart was racing. Then I closed my eyes for a few seconds and prayed.

God, can you hear my prayer today?
Why does Eric keep acting this way?
He always treats me like a throwaway,
and sometimes I just wanna run away.
I'm begging you—please send him today
to another planet near the Milky Way
or eleven light years from the USA;
that would really make my day.

If you won't make him vanish or go far away,
then this is my prayer on science fair day:
Help us to get along somehow, someway.
He has hurt me more than words can convey.
Yet I'm willing to forgive him, come what may.
Maybe you can teach him nice words to say,
so he can be my friend, not a bully, I pray.
Yes, I know it's a huge favor, any which way
but you can work miracles, night and day,
I trust that you'll be my strength anyway.
Just being honest with you today.
And there's another thing I have to say:
if we don't win the contest, God, it's okay.
But if the journalist decides that it's our day
to blow the rest of the competition away
with our creative food allergy display,
then we won't turn the prize away!

Connecting with God by combining prayer and poetry has always calmed my nerves. Feeling more comfortable, I decided to walk around and check out everybody else's tables. Besides our project, these were my faves:

- How many gummy worms does it take to clog your intestines?

- Will slime change color when heated to different temperatures?

- Does hand sanitizer kill bacteria, or should soap and water be used instead?

I made a special trip across the room to see Andy and Skylar's moldy bread experiment. They had created a simple display featuring five slices of bread. In front of each one was a label:

Slice #1

white bread

touched by nobody

after 10 days—no mold

Slice #2

white bread

touched by hands washed with soap and water

after 10 days—no mold

Slice #3

white bread

touched by hands washed with hand sanitizer

after 10 days—green and yellow moldy fingerprints

Slice #4

white bread

touched by dirty hands

after 10 days—dark green and yellow mold in large amounts

Slice #5
white bread
rubbed on a computer keyboard
after 10 days—black mold with a second layer of white fuzzy
stuff growing on top

I thought about all the times I'd shared computer keyboards in our classes and how *nobody* ever washed their hands before lunch—yuck! After seeing those nasty slices of bread, I decided to drink the *braaaain* juice and change my unhealthy habit. I pictured green, bacteria-infested mold growing over our computer keyboards and knew that from now on I'd have no trouble remembering to wash my hands with soap and water before lunch.

I walked back just in time to see the journalist approaching our table. My heart started to beat faster and my palms got sweaty.

"Hi, I'm Mrs. Penn," she said. "I *love* what you've done with your shirts—very creative!"

Ames was quick to say, "Thank you! My mom made them for us."

Mrs. Penn read our poster board and scribbled some notes on a sheet of paper before turning to the tablet. For the next few minutes, she watched our video and laughed hysterically every time toilet paper and bread were thrown. And every so often she reached into the cookie bowls to taste samples.

"These are delicious!" she said. "And that video is hilarious!" Nutty and I grinned at each other, hoping Mrs. Penn wouldn't notice.

"Please take as many as you'd like," said Ames, who didn't seem the slightest bit nervous around the journalist.

After eating a few more samples, Mrs. Penn left our table and headed over to the elephant toothpaste display. We overheard Eric, Jack, and Ryan explaining to Mrs. Penn how mixing certain chemicals can cause an oozing-foam reaction, like toothpaste being squirted out of a tube. They said it was going to be enough for an elephant to brush its teeth.

Apparently I wasn't the only one who'd been curious to see this experiment come to life, because a bunch of kids gathered around to watch Eric and his team mix ingredients, one by one, into a bucket. They added dishwashing soap, yellow and blue food coloring, and then a couple of other chemicals, explaining what they were doing as they went. When the last chemical was added to mix, green foam *exploded* out of the bucket! Kids were screaming and running for cover. The wet, gushing foam expanded by the second—like smoke from a rocket launch—covering the floor, tables, people, and anything that got in its way. There was enough elephant toothpaste for a *herd* of elephants! All the people in the vicinity—including Mrs. Penn and Mr. McCracken—were slipping and sliding everywhere.

A few hours later—after the cleaning crew had mopped up the chemicals and the firemen had inspected the building—everybody in town was talking about the science fair disaster. Unfortunately, several teams' projects were destroyed, including the electricity exhibit and the roller coaster display, but at least Mr. Green gave those kids A+'s on their science fair projects. Fortunately our project was saved since we blocked the cookies and tablet from getting covered in foam.

Eric's team was disqualified from the contest. What they'd failed to mention to Mrs. Penn when they were mixing the chemi-cals was that they'd *quadrupled* the quantities—*four* times as much as Mr. Green had approved. They'd wanted to wow the journalist with a big show so they'd win the contest. Well, they *did* make a big impression! Jack and Ryan were suspended for two weeks, and Eric was expelled. He'd already been suspended several times this year, and I overheard Mr. McCracken say that he was "tired of dealing with his shenanigans."

That night, I kept wondering, "God, was that you?" Eric and his friends had made a big mistake, which obviously had nothing to do with me. But I couldn't help but wonder…

Always end the day with a positive thought, no matter
how hard things were. Tomorrow's a fresh
opportunity to make it better.
— Zig Ziglar —

33

Life Goes On

A week had passed since the science fair disaster, and the contest winners had still not been announced. Everybody in our science class was excited to know who won, but Mr. Green just told us to be patient and to check this week's edition of *River Valley Magazine*.

Five minutes before my alarm rang in the morning, Hershey came into my bedroom and barked. The puppies needed to go pee-pee, so I grabbed my flashlight and brought them outside. Dusty did his usual thing—lifted a leg near the same dying bush—and Hershey took his sweet time sniffing wood chips near the kitchen window.

I shivered standing barefoot outside—the weather was definitely getting colder. So after Dusty finished doing his business, he bolted through the doggy door, hopped onto his bed, and snuggled up with his blanket. Hershey, on the other hand, was totally unaffected by the cold; with his thick coat of hair, he looked like a giant snowball with short legs and a swishy tail. I gave Hershey another minute in the backyard and then took him inside. The dogs cuddled up together, butt to butt, which made me smile.

Outside the kitchen window, the sun was rising over the mountains, and a yellowish glow covered every tree in the yard. I could tell that it was going to be a beautiful day.

I heard Kent leave for school, and then come back inside and slam the front door. "Hey, Louie, check it out!"

He came into the kitchen, grinning from ear to ear, and handed me the newspaper. Folded inside was a copy of *River Valley Magazine*.

"You guys won second place! Congrats!"

Not a hint of sarcasm.

And then, for the first time in my *entire life*, my brother high fived me. How do I describe the happiest moment of my life? It felt like the skies were raining miracles upon me! Eric could no longer bully me at school, Kent was treating me like a normal human being at home, and my best friends and I won second place in the science fair contest! I couldn't wipe the smile off of my face— *thank you, God!*

Even though we didn't win first place—Andy and Skylar won the trophy for their moldy bread experiment—I felt like I'd won the Lottery! I had two BFFs and a real brother.

Thinking about friends made me wonder if Nutty and Ames were up yet—so I sent them a group text: "Guess what? We won second place! Woohoo! We're on the cover of the magazine! Now we're in business!"

As I rode my bike to school, cold air blowing against my face, it dawned on me that I wasn't just thankful for the blessings in my life—I was also thankful for the painful parts. I considered my twisted life in middle school—sure, it could be stressful at times, but it was also pretty awesome! And I was thankful for the way things had turned out, knowing that God would always be there for me— *no matter what.*

Sometimes I just look up, smile and say,
"I know that was you, God. Thanks!"
— Anonymous —

~ The End ~

Write a Review

How did Louie Pickle's story affect you?
What did you like the most—his prayers, poetry, or food?
Help others to learn about anti-bullying by posting a book review.
When you write one sentence or twenty million and two
others will have the guts to talk about bullying too.
Speak up for yourself and others.
That's what you can do.
Thank you!

www.amazon.com/dp/1735085502

Contact Me

Virtual or In-Studio Tutoring Sessions
www.EurekaTutoring-SMILES.com
Since 2003

Kindergarten to 6th Grade
Reading, Writing, Language Arts,
Mathematics, Public Speaking

7th Grade to 12th Grade
Reading, Writing, Language Arts,
Note-Taking, Public Speaking

About The Author

As a child, Gina Wileman was fascinated with books and magazines—but she struggled with reading comprehension and dyslexia. This continued throughout middle school, where her grades declined and she was often bullied by a group of teenage girls. Despite social and academic challenges, Gina persevered and graduated from high school and then college (CSUN). In the process, she discovered that reading at a slower pace—visualizing the words and using her senses—greatly improved comprehension. Eager to share what she'd learned with other struggling readers, she opened a home-based business, *Eureka! Tutoring*.

Gina wrote this book to inspire students and adults who've dealt with learning issues, food allergies/intolerances, and bullying—at school or home—to never give up on themselves and to lean on God for support. She lives in California with her husband of twenty-five years, their adult son, and two shih-tzu pups. Gina enjoys preparing delicious meals and desserts for her family, all of whom have food sensitivities to either peanuts, gluten, or dairy. Her wacky cooking show, Whip-It-Up Wednesday, has been featured on Facebook and Instagram. This is her first of many books.

www.EurekaTutoring-SMILES.com

About The Illustrator

When Bob Longmire was born, the doctor put a pencil in his hand. It was the beginning of his lifelong passion for illustrating. He got over being bullied in school by making kids and teachers laugh through his doodles. After attending the University of Tennessee, Bob thrived as a designer in the ad agency world. He now works independently through Longmire Creative Services. An avid storyteller, he launched the Country Road Detours podcast in 2019. Bob gives thanks every day to God for letting his purpose in life be to make people smile and laugh through his artistic talents.

www.LongmireCreative.com

Acknowledgements

For those who have been bullied at school or home; for parental awareness, open-minded conversations, imperfect prayers, and forgiveness.

———— ◦ ◇ ◦ ————

For our loving God, who nudged me every step of the way to write this story. Thank you for trusting in me to share a message of hope.

For Paul, my husband, whose brilliant mind and sense of humor have intrigued me since the day we met; for his literary advice, honest feedback, and motivational tips during the past fourteen months. Thank you for your patience and guidance. I love you so much.

———— ◦ ◇ ◦ ————

For Conner, owner of my heart (gusto ko ang tawa mo) and talented-photographer son, who surprised me with a professional portrait to adorn the back cover of this book. Thank you, cutie. I love you more than the Earth loves the moon.

———— ◦ ◇ ◦ ————

For Sunshine, Pickle, and Ladybug… I will always love you.

———— ◦ ◇ ◦ ————

For Hershey and Dusty, our shih-tzu pups—therapy dogs for my tutored students—who snuggled near my feet nightly, while I wrote this story into the wee hours. I love you, Mr. Jealous Pants and Doodle Bug.

———— ◦ ◇ ◦ ————

For Momma, who said every page of my rough draft was her favorite; who listened attentively and laughed heartily, even when a chapter wasn't funny; who talked about holding my finished book in her hands constantly; and who supported my writing journey unceasingly. Thank you for having faith in me, beautiful lady. I love you.

For Daddy, who purchased our family's farmhouse in Woodstock, VA, where most of my favorite childhood memories began on that dilapidated, six-acre property near Stoney Creek; who encouraged me to become a writer like his father; and who graciously contributed to the production of this book. Thank you for the memories. I love you.

———— ◆◇◆ ————

For Donna-Lisa, my spirited 'wise owl' sister, who knew I would write and publish a book—even before I believed it myself; who urged me to join her virtual writing workshop in 2016, despite my hesitancy; who reminded me to just keep writing, even when I felt uninspired in 2019; and for the tears we shared while reading chapters 12, 13, and 14 together in 2020. Thank you for the goosebumps, sis. I love you.

———— ◆◇◆ ————

For Kristen Bennett-Chavez (ARTiculateEditing.com)—phenomenal editor—who dove into my story as if it was her own; who cared for the characters and scene development and then artistically rearranged sentences, like a symphonic movement; who was extraordinarily detail oriented, witty, and professional. Thank you.

———— ◆◇◆ ————

For Bob Longmire of Longmire Creative Services—funniest man on the planet and a great friend—who masterfully designed the book cover, beautifully formatted the manuscript, and whimsically crafted the illustrations; who poured his heart into this faith-based project, because it was meaningful to him too. Thank you for the endless laughs.

———— ◆◇◆ ————

For my tutored students—especially those who have been excited to read this book and have shown an interest in writing stories of their own—including Adeline, Adem, Alexis, Amiliah, Andy, Autumn, Brady, Christian, Christopher, Connor, Daelon, Daniel, Elizabeth, Ethan, Harper, Hayden, Jade, Jason, Jen, JJ, Joey, Jorge, Joshua, Julia, Kaelin, Kaliyah, Lily, Max, Melany, Mia, Morgan, Olivia, Preston, Robert, Ryan, Simone, Skylar, Sophia, Talayah, Taylor, Titan, Tootsie, and Vidal. Each and every one of you is special to me; I appreciate and adore all of you.

Made in the USA
Middletown, DE
11 November 2020